Dope Boy Magic 2

Chris Green

**Lock Down Publications and Ca$h
Presents**
Dope Boy Magic 2
A Novel by *Chris Green*

Dope Boy Magic 2

Lock Down Publications
P.O. Box 870494
Mesquite, Tx 75187

Visit our website @
www.lockdownpublications.com

Copyright 2020 by Chris Green
Dope Boy Magic 2

Lock Down Publications
Like our page on Facebook: Lock Down Publications
@
www.facebook.com/lockdownpublications.ldp
Cover design and layout by: **Dynasty Cover Me**
Book interior design by: **Shawn Walker**
Edited by: **Lashonda Johnson**

Chris Green

Stay Connected with Us!

Text **LOCKDOWN** to 22828 to stay up-to-date with new releases, sneak peaks, contests and more…

Thank you.

Submission Guideline.

Submit the first three chapters of your completed manuscript to ldpsubmissions@gmail.com, subject line: Your book's title. The manuscript must be in a .doc file and sent as an attachment. Document should be in Times New Roman, double spaced and in size 12 font. Also, provide your synopsis and full contact information. If sending multiple submissions, they must each be in a separate email.

Have a story but no way to send it electronically? You can still submit to LDP/Ca$h Presents. Send in the first three chapters, written or typed, of your completed manuscript to:

LDP: Submissions Dept
Po Box 870494
Mesquite, Tx 75187

DO NOT send original manuscript. Must be a duplicate.

Provide your synopsis and a cover letter containing your full contact information.

Thanks for considering LDP and Ca$h Presents.

Acknowledgments

First, I would love to thank Allah for giving me the strength to keep striving. Sometimes, things will get low in your life and you would surely need him to repaste things as you go. Cerenity, my beautiful, amazing, and direct young daughter. You are well equipped when it comes to learning, and progressing. You are my world, and I will continue to show you that by applying my actions daily. I love you more than words could explain.

I wanna thank my mama, brother, my entire family. I've become more silent with a lot of things because I realized that everything doesn't deserve a reply. It has taught me to grow, and measure situations perfectly. I can't wait until I'm home with you all.

To all my friends, Muslim brothers and close associates, I love you all whether you speak or even message me at all. No distance or time could change that love. It's embedded 4eva. I am author Chris Green. I'm here for a purpose and that's to supply my fans with their monthly dose of drama. I hope that you all enjoy and only a few of you truly know where this series is leading. Pay close attention, and flip inside of this masterpiece with patience.

Dedications

This book will be dedicated to the all-American basketball legend Kobe Bryant and his strong reflection Gianna Bryant. You guys story has ripped my heart to pieces and it pains me to see a tragic incident as this. My pain goes out to your family and I'm sure that you and baby girl will be accepted into Paradise for your loveable and righteous deeds. Your motivation will continue to rise through the upcoming basketball stars, and hopefully you will be able to see that we will not forget you two no matter how long the years by pass us.

May Allah Grant you and Gianna through the gates of his home. We love you.

Chris Green

Prologue

As the bullets ricocheted off Tipton's McLaren. Halo pushed him towards the floor before exiting the passenger door with his gun blazing viciously.

Pak! Pak! Pak! Pak! Pak! Pak!

The accurate slugs penetrated the side of their truck and one happened to find its home in the side of Skeet's head. The pistols in his hand crashed to the ground and his lifeless body hung from the window causing Dejuan to floor the pedal and evacuate the scene. Halo continued to fire his weapon at the vehicle until his clip was empty. The atmosphere of the street was in havoc and cars swerved recklessly to get away from the flying bullets. Halo wasted no time running back to Tipton's side.

"You okay, God?" He noticed the blood that was slowly seeping through his arm sleeve.

Tipton grunted in an aching manner before sliding out of the driver's seat. "I think so, just get us the fuck outta here.

Moving hastily around the car, Halo jumped behind the steering wheel causing a high shrill to release from the tires.

"We gotta find the closest hospital, God"

"Fuck that, no hospitals. Get us to the house and call Chocolate," Tipton ordered while gripping his arm.

Nodding with a heated expression. Halo began to accelerate on the gas. While Tipton rested his head against the seat. He closed his eyes, he never liked to reveal his thoughts when it came to delicate situations like the one, he was currently facing. Unfortunately, there was no choice.

"I want that bitch dead. Put the word out, I got fifty racks for Dejuan's blood. A hundred for whoever can bring him to me alive."

"Whatever you say, God," Halo replied before turning on

the interstate.

Chapter 1

"Fuck all that, he's running around this bitch like he, Mr. Untouchable. That boy got a whole family out here," Rex fumed as he paced around Tipton's living room, gun in hand.

"Understood, but they ain't the ones who shot at me. Try to calm down so we won't alert the entire neighborhood on what's about to take place," Tipton replied as Chocolate wrapped the rest of his arm.

"What the hell do you mean calm down? He just tried to kill you, idiot!"

"Watch ya fucking mouth. I know he just tried to kill me because I got the bullet in my arm to prove it. It's gonna get handled. Skeet, ain't around to help that coward ass nigga no more. All you gotta do is relax and let things play out. I don't know about you, but I ain't got another bid in me. So, if you ain't ready to eat beef and macaroni for the next twenty-five years. I suggest you go outside and take a chill pill like now."

"Yeah, I guess you know what's fucking best boss man." Rex walked out of the patio door.

Chocolate cut her eyes at Tipton and stood to her feet. "You can't fault Rex for the way he feels about this. The next time he tries anything stupid you might not be lucky enough to walk away, Tip. The longer he stays alive, the more he feels invited to come for you.

Tipton brushed off her comment as he stood to his feet. "Like I said, this foundation we built is bigger than, Dejuan. We either getting our money or we ain't doing nothing.

Chocolate shook her head and handed him two pain pills. "Money means nothing when a person you care for is at risk. Take those and try to get some rest. If you need me, call."

As she strutted past, Halo, she stopped to lock eyes with him. "If you're his true friend you'll talk some sense into him."

Chocolate's words snagged at Tipton's mind. Regardless of her spilling the truth. Critical problems caused for drastic measures. Every decision made was sure to be the best, and all things happened for a reason.

Sincere couldn't help but to speak, "What the hell are we gonna do about this drop? Kenny has been blowing my line up and I've run out of lies to tell this man. If we don't speed up the process. We might lose this deal," he informed with worry.

"My wife is upstairs sleep. I'd appreciate it if we can keep the tone of this conversation down," Tipton said as he focused on the cellphone in his hand.

"Nah, you need to bring this conversation up bro. You're the one always on my ass about this time schedule. We got shit to handle. By the way, my sister graduated with a three-point nine grade average. I can guarantee that she knows what you do for a living."

Tipton shook his head with a frown before rubbing his temple. "Y'all niggas need to learn some fucking patience. People don't get rich in the game for moving to damn fast. They come up from taking their time and thinking shit through."

Sincere shrugged his shoulders and brushed off the situation. "Let me find out my sister turning you away from this money? Me and Rex can slide around to let the workers know what's good. That should give you a few hours to snap out of this deep ass depression you in," he stated before heading out of the patio door.

"Why don't you just let me handle it, God?" Halo spoke with an unreadable facial expression.

"Because I'm not putting you at risk. If anybody gets a glimpse of you touching that nigga up. We both going down.

Check this, bro, business is not a movement that we can just put on pause because off a minor issue. The scars you place in this game will be the same ones you leave with. Let this shit run its course and watch how we remain at the top."

"Whatever you say, God." Halo tossed the shot of liquor back that rested in front of him.

Tipton spotted a message from Rika flashing across his screen and exhaled a sigh of relief. He looked over at Halo and smirked, before rising from the couch. "It's time."

****

Roswell Georgia wasn't a county that too many people wanted to be caught treading in. Being known for their ninety-five percent conviction rate would have the toughest killers in Atlanta on eggshells.

Halo glanced at the GPS on the dashboard, then stopped the rented Tahoe in front of a large two-toned brick home. Observing the private property sign clinging to the fence gave a clear indication for the unknown guest to keep it pushing.

"Maybe we got the wrong directions, God?"

"That's impossible, I typed it in the exact way she texted it to my phone."

Before he could reach for the touchscreen inside his pocket. A loud buzzing vibration erupted causing the gate to open. Halo glanced over at Tipton, shrugged his shoulders and pulled inside the narrow driveway. The beautiful home that rested in front of them easily ranged in the millions. Not including the three luxury vehicles that were parked by his four-door garage. After pulling the car up to the main entrance, both men stepped out observing their surroundings. Tipton's eyes couldn't help but stare at the Ferrari F12 Berlinetta. The hood was raised giving you a view of the 730-

horsepower engine. It was a devil dashing out at 0.62 miles in three seconds, and the metallic blue paint could cause you to think that you were staring into a glass mirror.

Halo noticed the elderly, black butler standing quietly at the front door. As the two reached the entrance of Sleepy's home. The Butler spoke with a light tone, "Good morning, Mr. White. The boss is waiting for you." He made his way into the house allowing Halo and Tipton to follow. After they crossed the threshold. He applied the locks on the door. "This way please."

Once he led them through the large corridor, he entered the living room announcing Tipton's arrival. "Sir, your guests are here."

The man rose from his chair and moved swiftly over to them with his hand extended. "I finally get to meet you face to face. The name is, Sleepy." He stood in front of Tipton with a calm posture.

His intentions were to speak back until he took notice of the plug's resemblance to him. Standing two inches taller than him. His hair sported deep waves and his Hugo boss two-piece suit was matching his smooth, brown loafers. His skin color sat an even tone and they also shared the same low, brown eyes. It made it seem as if Tipton was staring into a mirror instead of a man that he never met in his life.

"Rika has spoken highly of you. I never thought we would really get a chance to really link, but she tells me you share the same strength as your mother.

"And what would that be?" Tipton replied.

"Hustling of course".

Placing his attention on Halo, Tipton gestured for him to leave the room.

Sensing his friend vibe, he nodded and headed out with the butler directly behind him.

"Is there something wrong?" Sleepy asked noticing the slight movement.

"I think I should be asking you the same thing. Is there something I'm missing?

Knowing the questions could possibly be presented sooner or later. Sleepy took a seat motioning for Tipton to do the same. "I never thought that I would see you grow into a businessman so fast. Mary's sternness led me to believe that you wouldn't even be caught playing around in this game.

"That's not what I want to hear. Who were you to my mom?"

"I supplied her with the product".

What else did you supply her with?" Tipton questioned with a stern expression.

As he rubbed his goatee, Sleepy caught the remark, but decided to choose his words carefully, "There was a time that I was dating Mary. I met her down in New Orleans, on a business trip that I took every other week. I never knew that she was in a relationship, nor did I know she was dating Vel who worked for, my clientele. After she got pregnant, that dude acted like he couldn't control his hands. I asked her numerous times to let me help, but she continued to deny me. After I left for Atlanta, she hit my line a few months later alerting me that she was now in Detroit. That's where you was born. After having another run-in with, Vel. She finally took my advice and came to Georgia. She never looked back after that."

"So, you was fucking her too, basically," Tipton said being straightforward.

"I think we can use better words out of respect for your mother?"

"We can cut the bullshit. You look just like me. Unless that was something you didn't notice."

Crossing his fingers, Sleepy leaned back into his leather chair. "I asked Mary was it a possibility of me being your father. Every time I brought up this conversation, she would tell me, Vel was your dad. She was very discreet when it came down to our business. She wouldn't let anything come in between her getting that money. Not even you. It was the reason I felt that she was holding something from me. If you're asking me if I feel that she was lying? I guess that's kinda obvious, Tipton. There's a reason you're sitting in my home right now and it's definitely not just to pick up some weight. You're a man now. I can only tell you the truth from my side and hope that you accept it."

Tipton looked into Sleepy's eyes. He knew his words were solid as ice. The sincerity was pouring from his heart. He wasn't throwing up a smokescreen to hide anything. Neither was he oblivious to the way Tipton was feeling at the time.

"And I suppose Rika knew all of this, too? When I first met her. She said that I looked just like him. I suppose that him, was you?"

"Rika knows a lot of things. She's paid to stay in her place. Her job is to make us happy and push our product, that's it."

Tipton shook his head and rubbed his temple. "Trust me, she never seems to fail with that."

They shared a laugh, then Sleepy grabbed the set of keys off the desk, tossing them to Tipton.

"What are these for?

"Your vacation to Cuba. Go ahead and distribute your supply. Take a break for a few days. I know your fiancée and friends could go for a little change of scenery. Everything you need is already there. The beach house is set up and you'll have a car waiting for you once you arrive. Passports and everything on me."

"How did you know I was engaged?" Tipton asked with a

small smile.

"It's not much I don't hear or see. Let's just say that I'm your eyes to make sure things flow smoothly for you. Business will be handled, right here from now on. Rika will text you the directions to the house after your plane lands. Maybe if you're not too busy when you get back," Sleepy offered.

"Maybe." Tipton nodded before heading for the door.

After clarifying the new situation. He really understood the reason Sleepy was kept in the dark. It was the same reason his mother held her lucrative position. There were questions that weren't meant to be answered at the time. But there was some that definitely needed to be explained soon.

Stopping in his tracks, Tipton turned facing him before departing. "Have you ever thought about who crossed my mama?"

"Of course, but that would be me moving off my feelings, not facts"

Soaking in his remark, Tipton nodded before proceeding out of the home. After trailing through the parking lot. He made it back to the car where Halo sat behind the steering wheel.

"You a'ight, God?"

Looking at the black duffle on his back seat. He paused before responding, "I'm Gucci."

"Maybe it's just me, God, but dude in the crib look like he could be your twin."

"I thought I was the only one who caught that. It's kind of a perplexed situation.

What you think about taking a little vacation?

Halo raised a brow inquisitively. "Vacation, where?"

"The land of connections." Tipton smiled before they pulled away from Sleepy's home.

Chris Green

Chapter 2

2 Days Later

Trinidad: 4 Hours from Cuba

After traveling four hours away from Havana. Tipton and Janita eased down a cobblestone street where vibrant colors shined on every block. Their entire day was filled with scenery that rated the top twenty beautiful places to explore on the tropical wonderland. Enjoying a view of the Salto Del Caburni, a 210-foot waterfall. They caught a quick sunbathe on Playa An`con where his beach house was located. Hours after they rebooted with dinner at La`Redicc`ion. It was now nighttime on the edge of town where they shared a rememberable moment at the popular cave club, Disco Ayala.

"I'm gonna go use the restroom, then we can leave." Janita kissed Tipton before walking away from the bar.

He nodded his head and turned back to the counter ordering one last shot of coconut rum. As he bobbed his head to the Maraca shaking music that bumped loudly. His attention switched to a rough Cuban who took a seat directly next to him.

"Are you enjoying Cuba, my friend? Beautiful place, eh?"

"It's a'ight," Tipton replied in a nonchalant manner.

"What brings you to the West Indies? The Caribbean Sea is a long way from America." He smirked through broken English.

Having the skill to sense negative energy. Tipton decided to play his cards right to see where the conversation was headed. "The same reason you came and sat down next to me."

Smiling with a sinister grin, the Cuban snapped his fingers at the bartender. Moving quickly the man placed a bottle of

Verite La`Muse champagne on the countertop.

"My reasons could never be known. How does an ordinary man like me own one of the best clubs in Trinidad? Or how do I profit millions in a three-month run? It's called being consistent. Your look spells ambition in bold letters and that would be a good enough reason," The Cuban man spoke while refilling his shot glass.

"How much?" Tipton replied still looking forward as if the conversation wasn't being held.

"That depends on your range of spending."

Spotting Janita heading over to him, he stood to his feet. "I'm afraid that a number to contact you would have to do for now. It's about time for me to depart."

The Cuban pulled the business card from his pocket and placed it into Tipton's palm. "Try not to waste time. It's very valuable," he replied before glaring at Janita.

"Surely time is of the essence." Tipton placed a hand on his woman's back and led her towards the exit.

"What's his problem?" she asked as they headed through the small crowd.

"He was just ranting about investing in a load of goats or something. Just another foreigner trying to be American friendly."

As he watched the two depart from the club. The Cuban man grabbed his bottle of champagne and slid towards the private section of Ayala. He moved through a bundle of beads that hung from a doorway.

A white-haired man that puffed on a good Habana cigar looked up at him. "What did he say?"

"In due time, Sir. I know he's gonna cooperate."

Stopping the poker game at hand. The old man sat down his cards. "For your sake, you better hope so."

****

After walking into their lovely beach home, Tipton and Janita made their way inside the humongous living room.

"If it isn't Romeo and Juliet? I just knew y'all was gonna be out booty popping all night." Rex laughed before puffing on his stuffed joint.

"What's good, God?" Halo added, he was sitting next to Chocolate in front of a seventy-inch plasma.

"What's good? We a'ight, just getting a little bit of this Cuba life in our system. It's more beautiful than I thought," Tipton answered while pulling Janita down on the couch with him.

"Tell me about it. I did a little exploring today myself. My fine ass Cuban Teriyaki chicken should be here any minute now. I'm trying to dip that ass in soy sauce like four times before we leave." Rex looked down at his watch.

"You need a psychiatrist," Chocolate huffed.

"The last time I checked. I asked how much you charge?"

"Not in your deepest dreams, Mr. Platypus." She smirked arrogantly.

"I see y'all been getting along well?" Tipton chuckled.

"Not really. You took the key for the guest home so we couldn't get wasted and ignore, Peanut Brain over here. I'm tired of getting in that fishy ass water and watching Reruns of Empire."

Tipton glanced at his timepiece, then bobbed his head lightly. "Don't have a nervous breakdown. I'll run over there and grab a few bottles of something to drink. Roll up and try not to kill each other before I come back." He stood heading for the door.

When he stepped outside, a sharp gust of wind caused him to fold his arms as he moved hastily through the sand towards

Chris Green

the guest home. Cuba was definitely not the average residence. It was far away from the plain Jane city limits, but a short rest from the fast life was surely needed. The money was stacking faster than he could count it and Chocolate was the one to thank. All his coaching was paying off because she was doubling blocks faster than a two-year-old with a case of Legos. If all continued to twirl correctly on their tracks. He was gonna make everyone on his team a millionaire within the next year in a half.

After proceeding up the guest's home porch, he used the key to let himself in, closing the door behind him. He glanced around before continuing towards the wine collection that was stationed in the large kitchen. As he moved past the open living room, he paused.

Staring at him with her red legs spread eagle, Rika took a small sip of the Grey Goose that dangled in her left hand. Her intoxicating breasts hung freely from the beige cashmere robe on her body. Her sweet, smelling perfume lingered over to Tipton instantly giving him the hard head inside of his pants.

"Rika, what are you doing here?" His eyes roamed down her body curiously.

"Enjoying our vacation. It's hard for people like us to get some time off." She lifted from the couch and walked over to him, grabbing his swollen manhood. She smiled. "Very hard."

The hypnotizing Chanel number 5 was booming from her skin capturing his full attention. As he tried to step back, she moved forward and backed him into the corner.

"Tipton, could you do Rika a favor?" she requested in a begging manner.

"That depends, I was kind of in a rush." He inhaled deeply trying to think of his next excuse.

"I'm gonna bend over in that chair right there—and I want you to slide right behind here." She enticed him by spreading her ass.

"Don't do this to me, right now, Rika. My girl is waiting on me, I can't."

"Pleassseee!" She pouted her lips.

She slid her fingers down Tipton's stomach, eased into his polo boxer briefs and released his magic stick. Rika licked the tip of her hand before squatting down.

"You're so amazing," she whispered before opening her mouth widely.

****

Delano South Beach Florida

Finally arriving at the Soigne Penthouse Suites. Sincere carried
two large duffle bags through the entrance and headed straight for the elevator. After making it to the top floor, he proceeded towards Kenny's room and was stopped by a black muscular bodyguard.

"Where the hell you going, lil' dude?"

"I'm here to see, Quick." Sincere frowned from the hand that was placed on his chest.

The bodyguard glanced down at the bags in his possession. He opened the hefty sacks and looked inside. After frisking him thoroughly, he stepped to the side and opened the room door for him to enter.

"Fake ass John Coffee looking muthafucka," he mumbled before walking in.

"Sincereee! How are you? Come in, come in," Kenny said with a slur while mingling in his Jacuzzi with two blonde heads.

"I'll appreciate it if you can depart from the women for a

few seconds so we can handle our business."

After tonging down the women quickly, he climbed out of the water with a huge grin, pushing back his slick hair. He hugged Sincere around the neck. "It's about fucking time, I thought you mighta bailed out on old Quickie."

Kenny laughed before taking a seat in front of his oval-shaped table.

"Why didn't you tell me this place was guarded like a fucking army base? I saw three K-9 vans spread throughout the parking lot. I almost shitted on myself nigga. Wassup with that?" Sincere questioned with his leg shaking harder than a seizure.

Taking a bump of the raw cocaine, Kenny snapped his head back from the rush before replying, "Sincere, take it, easy kid. All these crooked, pork eating sons of bitches are on my payroll. I practically own the whole building. Powder your nose and let's have a drink." Kenny slid the plate across the table.

"No thank you, I need to get ready for this drive back to Atlanta."

"Everything is accounted for, your money is sitting in the corner. All Benji blue franks."

"Perfect," Sincere said cutting his eyes at the two women who started to fondle each other.

"So, when am I gonna meet the boss man? I don't think he understands how much dirty Paradise needs him? I can't manage this entire state by myself," Kenny mentioned before chugging down a cup of clear vodka.

"That would have to be something you set up on your own. All I do is bring you the product."

"That doesn't mean you can't earn the same salary, my friend. This dirty game is filled with many tricks for guys like us who actually want to touch the top. I see control over the entire south." Kenny pointed with an assuring finger.

"This is Tipton's car. It sounds great, but I'm not in control of how this boat floats," he replied before one of the naked snow bunnies climbed next to him.

Her olive skin glowed from the recent suntan including her flamingo pink nipples. He couldn't help but trail his pupils down to her heart-shaped vagina.

"I'm Cream. What's your name?" she asked with a curious grin.

"Sincere," he replied with a slight drawl as if he were drunk.

Her body smelled like she bathed in a tub of roses, and her white blondish hair wisped into her face from the patio breeze.

"Cream, what did I tell you about being so aggressive? Give the man some space will you."

"He's grown, Kenny. Let him speak for himself." She rolled her neck before turning back to him.

"You have to excuse her behavior. When the bitch gets a little candy in her system. She becomes a little overbearing. Maybe on the next visit, you can get a taste of South Beach and white cheeks." Kenny smiled.

Feeling the sexual tension steam off her body. The thought of having a night of relaxation crossed Sincere's mind. It had definitely been a minute since he played with some action. One day of fun couldn't hurt. Especially when the crew was experiencing the tropical life in Cuba.

"How much does it cost for a night around this place?" Sincere asked causing Cream to blush from ear to ear.

"When you're with me, it's always free." Kenny leaned forward and poured him a strong drink.

Chris Green

Chapter 3

Dejuan pulled into Vel's home, stepped out of the SUV and looked up into the serene sky. The day for him to rise in the game was finally presented. All he could do was picture spilling Tipton's blood over his new trophy. He rang the doorbell, Sonya answered and quickly led him to the dining room.

"There's a reason y'all niggas are a part of this shit. I put you in those streets for the same reason. It's time to tighten things up," Vel spoke to the few men that sat in front of him. All heads turned from the sight of Dejuan walking in and Vel folded his arms. "Everybody claiming they ready to put in work. Now would be the chance, and you damn sure don't receive them twice. Meeting adjourned," he announced watching the men stand to leave his home.

Dejuan slid past the moving men and posted near his side until the room was clear. "What was the point of me showing up if they were gonna peel when I walked through the door?"

"Because their mission ain't the same as yours. Play your position and let me worry about them. I explained what I need you to do and from a man of your caliber. That should be easy," Vel confirmed.

"Yeah, I remember. You want the nigga dead."

"If he chooses to keep disregarding our warnings again, and don't respect our wishes. Yes!"

"Good, because my mind was already made up with splatting the entire group. I need that money."

"That's fine, but before you get paid something has to be accomplished. According to you, everything was gonna be handled the first time. I guess we see how that turned out?"

"It's time to change that. If he doesn't listen, I'm killing everyone. Sounds reasonable, right?" Dejuan smirked folding his arms.

"Not everyone."

"What?"

"The dread head leave him alive. Don't touch him period," Vel demanded with authority. "Just relax and stay alert. I'm sending Sonya to get a little understanding. After that, you can do as you please."

Shifting his attention to the silent woman. He shook his head in disbelief. "You think she can do a better job than me with applying pressure?"

"Exactly," Vel answered before she smoothly slid out of the room.

****

After four days of the island life. Their normal routine was back in effect. Tipton was now pushing the packages for an even ten. The money Kenny was spending caused his weight to triple in a matter of weeks. Clientele in the sweet city wasn't an option. Using Chocolate's magic hands, and his expert wrists. The entire game would be at their feet.

Tipton stuffed the last five kilos into the Louis Vuitton tote bag, then passed it off to Rex's young worker. "That's ten in all. Make your plays and drop the rest off on, Chocolate."

"Word, I got you, big bro." He picked up the bag to leave.

As he took a seat next to Halo on the couch, Tipton smiled. "I gotta say, God. Shit is starting to look real good."

"I know right. That was the last of it that he just grabbed, and we ain't had that shipment more than a week. Another year or so, we will never have to see a Pyrex pot ever again. I had a few ideas for a café or something. I need to really sit down and form a blueprint."

"You're gonna prosper no matter how you choose to do it,

28

God. It was meant for you to be the leader of all this."

Tipton nodded in silence to Halo's encouraging words. "What about you, bro? You still ain't told me nothing you want to do with all this money we making."

Shaking his head with a stern expression, Halo brushed away the ridiculous plan quickly. "I'm just here to make sure you're safe, God. I'm a simple person which means I only got one position to play. People start to feel entitled when you open certain doors for them to see what you can really do. I know my purpose," he said with a smile before heading for the bathroom upstairs.

Leaning back against the couch, Tipton rested his eyes knowing that his close friend was spitting the truth. Only so much could be shown to a person before they started to feel you're obligated to spread your shit. It was the way of the world. Nothing would ever change but the people who were next to be born, and the ones who were placed in the ground. It was just a cycle and motherfucker's emotions were the rotation of the entire circle.

Feeling the silenced handgun press down against the top of his head. He looked up into Sonya's eyes who held one finger up to her seductive lips. "If you make me kill you. This entire trip would be in vain. I'll ask the questions and you'll answer. Is there anyone else here with you?"

"No," Tipton mumbled while trying to hold his composure.

"Do you remember me?

"It's kinda hard to say. I'm looking back with a gun pressed down on my head."

"Good, that lets me know that I have your full attention. I came to deliver a message and how you reply will result in me strangling you to death or putting a bullet through your brain. Vel is offering you the deal of a lifetime. That's to knock off all the competition inside Atlanta and make you very rich. You refusing to work with him is only causing a disturbance to his operation. I'm afraid that I have been paid to come and push a decision out of you, right now. This would be the time to speak," Sonya said humbly.

"If Vel wanted to say anything to me. He shoulda came himself. Just as I told him before, I would never give him the satisfaction of living off my hustle. I'm sorry, truly I don't owe anyone an apology but you. I never meant to lie."

"What are you talking about?

"About someone being in the house with me." Tipton smiled.

The hairs on the back of her neck began to rise after Halo raised his pistol. Jolting her body around, she fired a shot missing his head by an inch. Tipton watched as Halo caved a hard, right fist into her chin. She instantly folded like a birthday card before hitting the floor.

"I see where you get the name Halo from, bro. You're a fucking angel." Tipton jumped to his feet.

"What do you want me to do with her, God?" he responded while staring down at Sonya's unconscious body.

Vel was obviously making a statement by sending a woman to handle his business. Tipton was seconds from having his life taken, and the thought of her getting so close quickly changed his mind on releasing her. "Tie her up and start the car. I'm going to lock down this trap spot until I find out how this bitch found us."

It was only one way to beat a person like Vel at his own game, that was to play it with him.

****

Sonya cracked her eyes slowly, a sharp pain quaked

through the left side of her head. The slight dizziness faded, and her sight locked in on Tipton placing a fork full of sweet Thai stir fry into his mouth.

"Hey, Sleepyhead. Your name is, Sonya, right?" he asked never looking up from his dish.

Realizing that she was bounded to a chair at the kitchen table. Nervousness began to consume her body. Taking a seat next to her. Halo opened up a fresh Styrofoam tray of curry chicken.

"Are you hungry? You've been out for a few hours." Tipton asked while stretching his arms.

Ignoring the question, she stared into his face with a stale look, then cutting her pupils over to Halo. He raised a spoon of rice to her mouth as if she was a newborn infant.

"Fuck your food," she mumbled before spitting on his shirt.

He grabbed her throat forcefully and squeezed, causing the air inside her windpipe to shut off. Then he glared down at her with his blue eyes and applied more pressure. The fast shuffling of her feet could be heard under the table as she slightly urinated from his grip.

"Calm down, Halo," Tipton ordered before slowly standing up.

After releasing his hand from her neck. She began to cough violently. Tears welled in her eyes and her lips started to tighten in anger.

"Just kill me!" she screamed.

"No one is gonna kill you. I just wanna know what the fuck boosted your head to come looking for me. I thought you was a clean-up girl, like a servant or something," Tipton spoke.

"Well, you thought wrong. Cleaning up is my specialty and I ain't talking about washing dishes," she replied with an indirect threat.

Thinking back to the day he first entered Vel's home. She carried a Glock in the small of her back. It didn't strike his conscience that she was possibly dangerous, but the action that just took place a few hours back made her outburst pretty clear

"So, you're his bodyguard?"

"Killer, big daddy, it's a difference." She smirked.

Yawning, Tipton checked the time on his cellphone, before placing it into his pocket. "Is there some type of trophy you get for that? How much is this dude paying you to put your life on the line for him?"

"I'm afraid that information is classified. Just like your precious recipe, remember?"

"You're a CIA agent now, huh?"

"No, an eight-year veteran. Sergeant and two times marksman of the US Navy," she replied with a serious face.

"Not impressed, lil' mama. Next time you might need to do more shooting and less talking."

"Oh, really? Mighty funny you say that when your heart was racing like a bitch taking a twenty-inch dick after my gun touched your forehead. I'd probably be the best you've ever seen if you just let my hands free."

Smirking at her arrogance, he leaned against the table. "Meet, Halo, all of that bullshit you just named in one."

"He's not even black, especially with those blue eyes. Hand to hand, I'll break him to pieces."

Shrugging his shoulders, Tipton chuckled. "Maybe in a few days, you'll feel a little better. I think you're still drunk driving from that lick to the chin."

"She has a mean bluff game, God. We might need to pay that old man a visit," Halo suggested while following him into the living room.

"That crummy ass nigga is just desperate, bro. Now that

we got his little crash dummy. He's gonna pull some more dumb shit after he realizes she's probably dead. Like sending another fuck up on the same mission."

"Dejuan?" Halo guessed.

"Exactly! I got a meeting across town, keep your eyes on that bitch," Tipton warned before quickly sliding out of the front door.

Being sure to apply the locks behind him. Halo turned around to meet Sonya's demonic smile as she sat at the table. "It's just me and you know. How about you let me out these restraints and see who's the real true savage in the room? What do you say, big man?"

Cracking his head to the side, Halo flashed a wry smile.

****

It was less than forty-five minutes before the Italian Olive Garden restaurant closed. Just as Janita was about to stand and leave. She spotted Tipton standing at a distance with a charming smile. She returned his flirtatious grin. He moved towards the table and placed a soft kiss on her pleasant lips. The taste of her sweet peach gloss and the firm fitting Elle Saab mini dress, made it seem like meeting her for the first time again.

"I didn't think you was gonna make it?" She exhaled while grabbing one of his hands gently.

"Nothing is more important than spending time with you. There's a reason I asked you to marry me."

Blushing, she matched his lustful gaze. "You don't know how excited I am to be with a man like you, Tipton. When I was younger, I felt that it was just a fairytale for a woman to find her knight. A love and savior that would appear when all seems to be fatally failing. I was once that princess inside the castle until you made my dream a reality."

As he watched the waitress placed a piece of Cassatta Alla Siciliana in front of Janita. He placed two hundred dollars in her hand.

"Thanks, Tipton." She smiled before excusing herself.

"That was way too much money for her to be strolling off with. It's only a piece of cake baby."

"True, but it's not just any cake. She's the only one in this place capable of making it. Sponge cake, sweetened Ricotta cheese, and candied fruit that's bound together with chocolate buttercream icing," he said breaking a piece for her to eat.

Seeing her eyes glow in satisfaction, he laughed.

"Baby, this is delicious!

"Good, because she's the one who's making our wedding cake."

Janita leaned over and smooched his lips twice. "What did I do to deserve all this special love you're giving me?"

"When you accepted me as a husband. You gave me everything I needed. After you open your shop tomorrow. I'm gonna arrange for all your things to be moved to my place. You're my wife now. There's no point in being in separate locations. I'll feel more comfortable waking up next to you every morning." He brushed his fingers lightly down her cheek.

She couldn't help but smile at the man she chose to love forever. He was her true blessing. "Whatever makes you feel better my love."

'*Life is good,*' Tipton thought as he watched his wife enjoy her dessert. Family and friends were straight. Business was lovely, and envy was rising by the day. It was all part of coming up. No matter how much shit fluctuated. Losing was not in his line of vision. Even if that meant sacrificing himself.

Chapter 4

Peaches moaned lightly as she bobbed on Dejuan's manhood, saliva spilled from the side of her mouth. She stroked his shaft up and down causing him to lean back and puff on the hypnotizing marijuana as she handled her business. Feeling the sensation of her tongue gliding back and forth caused him to release an explosive orgasm down her throat.

Shittt," he grunted gripping a handful of hair until she swallowed every drop.

"Can I hit that blunt?" she asked wiping her lip.

He reached over to grab a cigarillo out the nightstand and tossed it on the floor. "Roll yo' own shit."

She smacked her teeth and mugged him. "I'm not a fucking dog, nigga. You can treat me with some respect."

"What is there to respect bitch?"

Ignoring the crooked ass remark, she started breaking down the cigar slowly.

"Have you thought about the plan I put in place?"

Peaches remained silent from his question and continued to pearl the blunt of weed.

"You a mute now, huh?" Dejuan spat.

"I can hear very well, Juan. I asked you to give me time with that. You think it's just easy to let you kill my baby daddy? Plus, I gotta help. What about, Kimmi? She needs him."

"I guess yo' life don't mean nothing?"

"What are you saying, Dejuan?"

"Let me be a little more clear on what I mean."

He tapped the blunt out on her mattress. Then landed the first punch to her temple causing Peaches to ball up. His fists rained down forcing her to scream.

"When I say do something. I fucking mean that shit!" He

yelled while striking whatever open space he spotted.

"I'll do it, Juan! I'll—do—it," She stuttered while he landed more vicious blows to her stomach and breasts.

Hovering over her with his nostrils flaring. He pointed a stiff finger. "That's what I thought you said. I don't know if you understand this, but I'm not your weak ass baby father. My word is the last word. That means ain't shit up for discussion."

"Tipton doesn't trust me! He won't even tell me where he lives. What do you expect me to do?"

"I expect you to do whatever the fuck I tell you too." Crouching down, he placed a hand gently on her chin. "I'm the one who cares about you. Not him, if he did, you would be next to him instead of behind. He's the enemy, not me. I shouldn't have to do this in order for you to see."

Blinded by the fake love, and deceitful hatred for Tipton. She couldn't help but to accept the new status of her life. It was either him or her.

"I'ma help you, Daddy. Whatever you want me to do." She looked up into his eyes with sincerity.

"Good." He smirked before dropping his shorts to the floor.

****

Tipton pulled into Sleepy's large estate, parked the 2018 Dodge Durango and stepped out. The early morning breeze was starting to simmer as the sun started protruding from behind the clouds. He walked over to the front door and prepared to touch the doorbell. Before his hands could reach the button, the door was opened allowing him to enter.

He observed the butler standing quietly to the side, then chuckled. "You have great timing."

"Indeed, Sir," the butler replied dryly.

Proceeding inside, everything Tipton laid his eyes on, spelled an obsessive amount of money. Sleepy's home reminded you of a clip from the movie Scarface. From his French oak floors, down to the neutral colored flex form furniture in his living room. His fascinating car collection was worth double times the yearly salary of the president. Not including the midnight black Bugatti that was stored in the two-car garage in the back.

As Tipton walked into the medium size dining room. Sleepy sat at the ten-foot table occupying a stocks and bonds magazine. Looking up to see him in his presence. Sleepy stood to his feet.

"I'm glad you make it. Hopefully, I didn't intrude on your business schedule?" He smiled before embracing him.

His Stefano Ricci suit was fitted to perfection, and the Pierre Corthay dress shoes on his feet cost an easy five thousand. "Are you hungry? I had breakfast made so we can eat while discussing business." He pointed to the delicious set up that covered the marble top.

"It's never a problem when business is in the conversation and I can never turn down any breakfast." Tipton took a seat in front of his plate.

Sitting on the opposite side, Sleepy slid the magazine across to him. "Do you know anything about that?"

Staring at the cover, he shrugged. "A little, I've never really been into the whole wall street thing. I try not to straggle off course on what I'm good at."

"You're actually straggling if you're not learning and paying attention. The same tricks that sleep with the trade game is similar to your hustle also. Just not in the same form."

"I don't think drugs can be placed in the same range as that. With my work, I get my bread on hand."

Sleepy smiled and sipped his coffee smoothly. "Really? With stocks you invest your money into something you feel will double overtime, maybe even quadruple. The same with the drug game. You spend your money on product that you feel is good enough to bring back your funds. They both share one common thing, timing."

Tipton sat down the fork and tuned into the knowledge being spilled.

"Everything we do whether legal or against the law. There needs to be perfect timing. I've officially made three out of state clientele's free agents, which means they belong to you now. I've invested money, time, and effort with building my reputation beyond the walls of Georgia. Now it's time to trade and place my investment in another hand of authority. You," Sleepy stated with a stern expression.

Maintaining his business posture, he folded his arms. "Why me?"

"Because your hustle is impeccable. It's not hard to do what we do, but it takes a brain to control the balance of negative and positive. Shifting too much could cause everything to fumble. There's only one other person I would put in this position, but that's not gonna happen." Sleepy shifted his eyes to the ceiling.

"Why?" Tipton asked curiously.

"Because she's not with us anymore."

Knowing that he was referring to his mother. He couldn't help but contemplate the offer. Everyone vouched for his mom's outstanding skills but meeting those standards was starting to seem impossible. The thought of expanding any bigger would mean more help, More eyes. It was a risk, but what wasn't a risk when it came down to the drug world?

"What you need me to do?"

"Expand, you're the only person I know that can pull a

double up with supply in less than two weeks. That along with your new connections you'll be guaranteed to see millions in no time. I'm dropping your prices to eight a key. The same deal that pushed your mother through the roof."

Feeling a sharp pain run through his chest after hearing the numbers. Tipton wiggled a finger in his ear. "Did you say eight?"

Before Tipton could reply, Rika stepped across the threshold. A pair of red Victoria Secret boy shorts hugged her round behind. Her breasts were barely covered with a red Tommy Hilfiger sports bra, and the curls she rocked days before were replaced with a set of attractive red dreadlocks.

Watching his eyes stitch to her backside, she grabbed an apple from the refrigerator making sure her monkey print could be displayed for him. "Good morning, Sleepy. If you don't mind, I would like to borrow him for a minute after you're done?"

He cut his eyes over at Tipton who sat with a clueless face, then cleared his throat. "Sure Rika, I'll send him right up after were done."

She gazed at him Tipton with nasty seductive thoughts and quickly departed.

"Thanks for offering me to the slaughterhouse. That girl is gonna fucking kill me."

Shaking his heads with a laugh, Sleepy stood from his chair. "Rika is very persistent, that's a situation I can't help you with."

Hearing the doorbell signal, he checked his Richard Millie timepiece. "Speaking of being persistent, I have someone for you to meet."

The house butler stepped from around the corner as if he was waiting for Sleepy to make his statement. "Sir, your guest has arrived."

The frail white man who appeared behind him carried a leather briefcase in his right hand, a pair of square round frame glasses covered his small, round, beady eyes, and his shirt was tucked neatly into his Hugo Boss dress slacks. "Tipton, I'd like you to meet Demon."

"Pleasure," the man uttered holding his hand out in front of him.

"Demon, what type of name that is for a lawyer?" Tipton questioned with a strange look before accepting his handshake.

Sleepy smiled and placed a hand on Tipton's shoulder. "He's not a lawyer. He's always assisted me over the years, and I place my full trust in him. He'll be here for you twenty-four hours, five days a week."

Scratching the side of his head in confusion, Tipton smirked. "I don't understand."

"Let's just say he's here to dispose of all your troubles"

****

It's crazy how you say you're a fucking killer but sit in the corner all day quiet like a bitch," Sonya spat staring into Halo's eyes.

The torment of her disrespectful words was starting to cook his blood, and if Tipton didn't arrive back in time. She was probably gonna receive a bullet to the center of her head.

"When I was in the Navy, all the boys with pretty eyes like you were either Chefs or gay. Now that I think about it, you do look familiar." She giggled.

He jumped off the couch, grabbed the back of her chair and pulled it towards the garage door.

"Where are you taking me to Macho man? It's too hot to be sitting a bitch outside. Did my words hit home baby?"

40

He dragged her inside the spacious parking room and released the restraints from her body. Then he took a step back and rolled his neck side to side, feeling her heartbeat increase. Sonya shook her way out of the ropes. "You're gonna be the first man I make beg for mercy."

Halo removed his shirt just as she stood to her feet. Before he could throw up his guard, she landed a vicious blow to his nose. His chest flared in anger. She dodged his left fists and received a quick uppercut to the stomach.

"Ughhhh!"

He grabbed her legs, slammed her aggressively into the wall. Then she scrambled to get up. He smirked as she started swinging recklessly. He caved a hard right to her rib cage. She panted before kneeling over in pain. Looking up into his eyes. She flinched after his hand cocked back to strike again.

"Go ahead, hit me! It feels good to beat up a girl doesn't it!" she yelled with a shaky tone.

"That was a quick fight for someone with a big mouth," Halo stated before turning to pick up the rope.

He curled her leg around his foot. She turned pushing him to the floor and climbed on top of him. She placed two punches on both his cheeks.

"Does that make you feel better?" Halo asked tasting the blood on his tongue.

Holding his neck, she stared into his sky-blue pupils. Her mind said to murder him, but the seat of her panties was speaking differently. His muscular frame felt as if she were sitting on a brick wall instead of a man. Not to mention the unique tattoos that covered his bright red skin. Knowing that he could easily break free. She cut those chances by placing a passionate kiss on his lips. Then she slightly arched her ass and slid a hand down to his stiff manhood.

He grabbed her wrists in a swift motion, quickly flipping

her over. Staring down, he watched as Sonya's body wiggled with lust.

He reached past his arms, she unbuttoned her pants, and slid them down to her thighs, undoing his zipper. She rolled over onto her stomach. Her beautiful, bubble-shaped behind gently bounced causing Halo to release his piece through the fabric boxers. He pressed Pressing two fingers on her love button. He twirled them forcing her to ride his rhythm. Her mocha, brown skin screamed gorgeously, and the wetness of her kitty felt like she was ready to release a massive flood.

While he stroked his erection. Sonya looked back into Halo's eyes just as he started to slide inside. Before she could moan from his length. He covered her mouth with his hand.

****

Moving around the floor of her painting shop, Janita shook hands with her potential customers that viewed her art for the past two hours. After the bids were placed. The portraits were sold completing the success of her first exhibit. It was a beautiful experience for the beginning of her career. Not including some important faces that sat throughout the auction. After the crowd slowly dispersed from the building, Janita's eyes landed on Peaches who still occupied one of the guest seats.

"Is there anything that I can help you with ma'am?"

Standing from the seat, she glanced around before closing the small space between them. "These are some nice paintings. Did you do them all yourself?"

Janita smiled and nodded.

Peaches frowned placing her attention on the remaining art pieces. "How much is all of it worth?"

"Excuse me?"

"These little drawings that you do? Are you making real money from this? Can this take care of you and your little boyfriend for the rest of your life?" Peaches asked before sparking her cigarette.

"I don't think that's any of your business unless you're trying to purchase the rest of my gallery. Just from this conversation, I can tell that's not about to happen. This is a no-smoking environment, and the exhibit is closed. Not to be disrespectful, but I'm gonna have to ask you to leave."

Blowing out the smoke from her cancer stick, she snickered. A devious smile spread across her face. "Is this the way you treat all of your customers? When I sit back and look around. I realize all of this crap isn't worth a penny, but you do have something that's worthy. Everything is not what it seems to be when you're in love pumpkin. Be cautious of your surroundings," Peaches warned.

"Is that a threat?"

"No, it's just advice. Try using it." She grinned before turning on her heels to leave.

Chris Green

Chapter 5

Tipton parked his car in the driveway and stepped out as Demon pulled his vehicle directly next to him. "You have an extraordinary home. I don't think I would've found this without following you." He smiled opening his truck door.

Tipton glanced at his crib before smiling. "I knew this house would serve a purpose one day. Great location, luxury look. It's the perfect home to start a family," he mentioned before reaching his front door.

"Indeed, Sir."

As Tipton walked inside, he paused with a confused expression after locking eyes with Halo. Sonya was snuggled at his side with a lustful smile plastered on her face.

"What up, God? I think she's ready to help us now." Halo motioned for her to sit up.

"Sounds like a start," Tipton replied ready to get more insight on Vel.

If they were able to hear the right piece of information. The problem was surely going to cease.

"First of all, I just wanna let you know I'm only doing this because of your steel body friend, right here. He's magical with his touch so count that a blessing, Mr. Dope Man," Sonya said with a slight attitude.

"Spare me the details. "What do you got for me?" Tipton dismissed her remark.

Demon held his position at the front door as she began to spill the beans.

"First of all, Vel is striving off another motherfuckas check. He's in major debt with some foreigners and his ass is on borrowed time. That's the reason he's trying to put you in the chokehold. He knows you're just like your mother with cooking. He estimated that if you help him using your method.

The enemy could be paid off within the next six months."

"How much does he owe him, Goddess?" Halo asked smoothly.

"Three-point-five million."

As he whistled, Tipton folded his arms. "That's a damn shame, but I don't have anything to do with that. I want to know when did I come into the picture? How did this nigga even find me?"

"Duh nigga, Jackson. He's been working for Vel forever. He wasn't nothing but a mere slave for whatever he was told to do. Vel already knew about your whereabouts before you came home," Sonya confirmed, her look was telling him that shit was beyond serious.

Tipton's mind scrambled to process the stupid information. It was always like a family member to come along and pull some slime shit along the way of a money rise. "Where the fuck is, Jackson?"

"He's dead"

Feeling a tingle flow through his body from her words, he frowned. "What?"

"Vel shot your uncle in the head a few days back. That's the reason you haven't seen him."

Halo's face tightened from conversation. The problem could simply be handled, and he was tired of sitting back waiting to be ended by Vel's conniving ass. "God, you gotta snap out of the zone you in. We can't keep sparing this man. If all this is true, we're sitting ducks waiting to be popped."

Raising a finger for silence, Tipton took a minute to reflect on his uncle. The sound of his name being mentioned with the word dead sent the same chills from his mother's death through his body. His fate was sealed when he crossed his flesh and blood. The only thing Tipton was sure about was protecting what he built with his life. No matter how deep the game seemed to be getting. "So, what's his plan? I'm not giving him the recipe. So, what's next?" He glared into Sonya's eyes demanding an answer.

Sensing his thick energy, she laid it on him uncut. "He's gonna come until he get what he wants. Vel is a dangerous ass nigga. He may seem to be slow, but there's always shit up his sleeve. Shit that he wouldn't even tell me about. You have to get him and make your move without being seen. He has eyes everywhere and one slip will result in everyone dying. That's the truth," she said before leaning back.

The living room fell into a dead silence for a slight moment. Tipton was so accurate when it came to making decisions that he didn't want to speak before his mind was made up. "I got a plan. It's gonna take your help, though. I'll pay you if necessary."

A sneaky smile formed on Sonya's face from his statement. "As long as Halo's added in the deal, I wouldn't care."

"Good, because if you're with us. There's no such thing as turning back," Tipton warned with a stiff expression.

"I don't mean to get off subject, but who the fuck is this guy, God?" Halo was pointing a finger over to Demon who stood quietly.

Tipton gave a thumbs up indicating that he was surely official. "He's gonna make a great addition to the team. He's no different from you, bro."

As the two killers eyed each other, their heads nodded as if it was a mutual agreement.

"Whatever you say, God. Maybe he can show me a few tricks when the action starts?"

"Indeed." Demon smirked.

****

Tipton stirred in his sleep from the sound of his iPhone buzzing. He fished his hand through the sheets with his eyes closed. After locating his cellphone, he answered in a groggy tone. "Hello?"

"Tipton!" Janita spoke through the phone as if she was nearly in tears.

Rising up in the bed, his heart began to quickly pace. "Nita, what's wrong baby?"

"My shop, it's gone," she whimpered weakly through the line.

"Sweetie, what are you talking about? What do you mean your shop is gone?"

"The last of it is in flames, someone burned it down!"

"What!" Tipton jumped from the bed as if the fire was up under him. "Baby stay, right there, I'm on the way."

"Please hurry."

Tipton hung up the call, quickly slid on his white Calvin Klein sweat suit and a pair of white puma slides. Then tucked a small Ruger 9 pistol on his waist. He grabbed his car keys and rushed out of the door. The entire drive, Vel's sinister face was running a mile a minute in Tipton's head. It was surely smoke when he appeared on the scene as if he wanted to extort someone out of what they'd worked so hard to build. Not to mention him taking the fake approach of wanting to be a recovering father that had been missing since a nigga first broke free from the pussy.

There was no other explanation for the cowardly stunt. When a message was trying to be shown. It was always the obvious snake from the bunch who was doing the showing. Real ones had no time to speak or show because they were too busy putting in action. The one thing he was for sure was if shit added up to Vel making the dumb ass mistake. The smoke was gonna show up at his front doorstep.

Ten minutes later, Tipton was pulling his Durango down the blocked off a section of the incident. Fire trucks aligned the sidewalk and he could see Janita standing to the side with the reporting officers. He parked his whip across the street from her gallery, stepped out and proceeded over to them.

"Baby, are you okay?" He embraced her into a tight hug.

"Tipton, they found gas cans behind the building. It was an arson. What would make someone do this?" Light tears slid down her face.

He wiped her face and kissed her lips. "Don't worry about nothing. We'll get another shop, bigger and better. I'm gonna get to the bottom of this, but I don't need you stressing."

While Tipton tried his best to ease Janita's pain. Detective Sandra Elliot locked eyes with him as she walked over towards the couple. "Mr. White, it's been a while. Can I have a word with you, Sir?" Her arms were crossed, and she gave him a distasteful frown.

"Give me a minute, Nita," he mumbled before stepping over to the pale-skinned woman. "What is it?"

"I'm not positive, Mr. White, I never knew you were married. So, it kind of confused me when we found out about the ownership of this property. This was something personal obviously. I mean you don't have random art gallery's getting burned down on the regular." She looked into Tipton's eyes waiting on a response.

"You're saying this because?"

"Because it seems like someone's out to get you. First your aunt, now your wife's painting shop. Are you sure there's no bad blood out there that authorities need to worry about? This is for the safety of your wife and yourself."

Tipton smiled in order to hold his composure. "This musta been a few street thugs that had nothing else better to do. I don't have any problems period. I'm sure there will be no issues. My insurance company will be able to clear everything up without a hassle."

"I see," Detective Elliot replied before pulling out her card. "I gave you this the first time and never got a chance to hear from you. Your aunt's case is still open and I'm getting a feeling that I need to start digging a little harder. I'm sure something is gonna show soon. I found out that you took her to a rehabilitation center days before she was murdered. Maybe it was something that transpired before they released you from prison?" She smirked.

"Maybe, I'm sure my three lawyers are working on finding out their own information also. Just in case someone's trying to plot any crooked turns or plans. I'm sure between your people and my answers will come soon. Will that be all detective?"

As they stood in silence, they held eye contact for a second before she proceeded back to her unmarked car.

Tipton, what did she say?" Janita asked with an inquisitive expression.

"She's just trying to do her job a little too damn good. I guess they have to interrogate everyone on sight until they find the most suspicious."

"That's strange, I've never seen officers so calm about a matter like this. It's literally five minutes away from a police station. There was a weird girl that showed up to my exhibit last night. She was looking at all the pictures and asking crazy questions about us. I think she threatened me," Janita made him aware.

"What, why didn't you tell me this last night?"

She stuttered and shrugged her shoulders. "I didn't think it was that serious. I asked her to leave and she left."

All Tipton could feel at that moment was rage. Vel was

50

playing a dangerous game that was about to spill a lot of innocent blood. There were boundaries that weren't meant to be crossed, but the rules were now off-limits.

"Go ahead and wrap it up here with these people baby. After you file the report for the insurance company come straight home." Tipton kissed her forehead.

"Okay," She exhaled and hung her head low."

"Hey," he spoke lifting her head with his finger. "You're a winner. My Queen doesn't have to win because you already won. Never let them see us sweat, no more tears."

"I love you, Tipton," she agreed with a nod.

"I love you more."

Watching her disperse back over to the scene reporters. Tipton dialed Halo's number before climbing back into the front seat of his car.

"Wassup, God. Do you need me?"

"Playtime is over, go ahead and start that process. I have to handle some business across town, and I'll be dropping back in right after."

"Whatever you say, God." Halo ended the call.

Tossing the cellphone into his cupholder. He pulled away from the cop infested street. Being in the game meant that losses would come, and sacrifices would have to be made. Tipton was prepared for both, a great mind was something that didn't come naturally. In order to play in the league. You had to possess the skills. Vel was surely going to be a witness for that shit.

Chris Green

Chapter 6

After making a few business calls to his lawyers. Tipton arrived in the Gwinnett county city limits within thirty minutes. Even though his mind was set on revenge. He had to remember that business overweighed feelings. The disrespectful matter was gonna be handled with precautions, and if it was meant to get ignorant after the chaos erupted. Bitch ass niggas would be executed with no mercy.

Arriving at his destination. He pulled into the open gated home and shut off his engine. A few white men occupied the front porch, and the guns that were laced around them made it clear that this wasn't the average Caucasian family.

As he climbed up the small stairs, he was greeted by Grim. The doorkeeper. A picture of a rattlesnake squeezing a mouse was tattooed on top of his shaved head. His skinny frame was not to be taken lightly, neither was his bushy mustache. His image resembled a kindergarten school- teacher and most would let their eyes deceive them. Not only was he skilled in physically beating someone to death, but his trigger finger had a problem when it came to controlling itself. He was the cousin of a made-man. It was more of a reason to join the family business.

"Tipton, long time no see bud. I'm guessing you're here for what?"

Ignoring Grim's slick tongue, he placed his hands behind him." Where's, Logan? Tell bro' I'm here."

Pulling roughly on the filtered camel cigarette. Grim exhaled before spitting over Tipton's head into the grass. "He's in the living room just walk through the door."

Remembering what was at hand, Tipton crossed the thought of negativity out his mind and continued inside.

The truth about a gun dealer was hard to understand unless

you knew one personally. The inside of their homes smelled like gun powder, and sandwiches and dirty Pit bulls were possibly laying around his domain, and more than likely, there was one freaky chick that all the bum ass drug dealers feasted on like the last Hawaiian sweet roll.

Logan was different, he was a preppy white kid with the heart of a ten-foot polar bear. He meant what he said, and never spoke twice on the same situation. Money was never a problem, especially when you were selling a quarter of Georgia all the murder weapons. He was the man to go to for anything, such as knives, guns, and armor. It was better than a one-stop-shop. He was like the light that never cuts off in the Super 8 motel.

As he sat at the table cleaning the inside of a desert eagle handgun, Logan looked up to see Tipton in front of him. "It took you long enough. You called me an hour ago. Being late is something I don't like man. It ain't nothing new with me, bro."

"I ran into a little trouble with my family. I'm always aware of how things operate. I need a package deal on something, and I need armor, a lot of it."

Logan gave Tipton a sly smirk, then he leaned forward. "Have you gotten in some trouble or something? I mean you know I haven't heard from you since Shaggy was murdered. Now you're here in my home asking for guns."

"If you're not processing shit correctly. I was still locked up when that shit happened. I'm still pondering on that same thing and I'm damn sure doing my own investigation to see who I can find."

"Oh, yeah, and how's that coming?"

"I got a few people in mind. Before they can find out that I know. Their ashes will be getting spread throughout the Pacific Ocean," Tipton replied with a straight face.

Logan sat the weapon down and wiped his hands with the dishrag next to him. "What do you need?"

"At least ten, including the armor."

"What are you trying to do, rob a bank?"

Tipton remained silent and watched as Logan stood to his feet. "I'll do it, send someone through in about an hour. It'll be ready then."

Tipton handed him a wad of cash and headed for the door. Before he could leave, Logan stopped him.

"Tipton? Shaggy was like my brother. You are, too. Certain forces aren't meant to be fucked with. A deep black cloud is about to rain over Atlanta for this mishap. There's a lot of unhappy people scouting for guilty faces, stay woke."

"Sure thing, Logan."

As he peeled out of the home, he walked down the steps past Grim, stopping to look at him. He flashed a bright smile. "Just to let you know, if that spit would've touched me a little. It would've been a mistake that was never forgiven," Tipton threatened before climbing in his car to leave.

****

Two Hours Later

Hearing the sharp knock on his office door, Vel sat his burning cigar down in the ashtray. "Come in."

As he looked into the eyes of his young runner, he could sense that something was wrong.

"Yo' Vel, you might need to come and see this shit."

He placed his handgun on the hip and headed out of the office to the front of his home. His cigar pumped thick smoke through the hallways until he made his way inside the family room. The rest of his men stood around clueless and Dejuan sat on the couch with his foot hiked up on the wooden coffee table as if he was running shit.

"What's the problem?"

Stretch slid the brown box on the floor towards Vel. His workers stood to the side with stupid grins.

"What the fuck type of game y'all playing? What is this hide and seek?" Vel snatched the latches open to see what was inside.

He reached in and his hand removed a large American flag that was folded into a neat triangle. The dog tags and black army fatigue suit he removed next sent bubbles flying through his stomach. The sight of blood on Sonya's property was a clear indication that the hit didn't go smoothly as he planned.

Vel's lips began to quiver in an angry manner. His hands began to tremble before he spoke, "Where in the fuck did this shit come from!"

"Someone dropped it off in front of the house about ten minutes ago. I thought it was a package delivery or something?" a young hustler admitted.

Looking at the man with a stupid grin, Vel walked over to him. "You thought that a packaging company just dropped off mail in front of the home? And you didn't think to stop these folks and see who the fuck they were?" His silence was the answer and it angered Vel even more. "If any of you niggas got a fucking brain. You'll have this nigga, right here slumped in a trashcan by tonight, and y'all will get on your job with bringing this nigga's ass to me. I don't care what it takes!" he yelled with Sonya's army tags clutched in his hand.

It didn't take long for the men to grab the new rookie kid and head out of the home. Vel was big on action so his words could make the ground shake from underneath anyone.

Rising from the couch, Dejuan approached him slowly, looking down at Sonya's property in Vel's hand. He chuckled.

"I warned you before you sent that bitch, bro. That nigga ain't dumb, and whoever that dickhead ass nigga is that he got with him is popping shit before he asks questions. Tipton is a thinker, you can't just push the button and expect him to fold. His heart is too big, expect the unexpected," he spoke with assurance.

"Now is not the time for explaining who did what. All I want is this nigga's operation on my fucking desk. He took mine, so I want all his taken. If he's moving sloppy like this, kill all they ass until he complies."

"If you allow me to handle this accordingly. I'll have him begging at your feet. There's one thing Tipton loves more than anything in this world. Patience will show you what I'm talking about." Dejuan formed a sly smile waiting for Vel's response.

Raising his hand with Sonya's dog tags. He shook them lightly. "I want blood for my girl. If you can make it happen you get it all."

"Done." Dejuan tossed the deuces before leaving Vel to himself.

The time for the trickery was now in effect. Tipton wanted an enemy. Now he was gonna feel exactly what the fuck wishful thinking could get a person. Dejuan only had his mind focused on one thing, Kimmi.

****

Sincere stepped out of his car with the new shipment and used his key to get inside of the north side trap spot. Finding Chocolate inside of the kitchen. He placed the huge bag on top of the table. "Excuse me, is there a reason why you didn't answer when I clearly explained that I was on the way with his shit? Now if some shit was to happen you would be the first one trying to cop pleas with Tipton."

Chocolate smacked her teeth, sat down the glass pot and placed the cooked dope under the stove vent. "First of all, I told yo' bum ass what I was doing before you prepared to bring your frogger looking ass over here. I been up whipping this shit since early this morning and I didn't feel like slowing down to coach you on bringing your slow ass over here. It's common sense," Chocolate spat before she searched through the supply thoroughly.

"You need to cut that fake ass Puerto Rican princess shit out. I'm tired of making dry ass trips to all these spots and I'm left handling the baggage job for all y'all slacking ass motherfuckas. All you have to do is answer the phone."

"Fuck all that nigga, let ya balls down and quit crying. This is only thirteen, Tipton told me it was fourteen. So, where is the rest of it?"

Giving her an annoying look, Sincere prepared to leave. "That's what he gave me, Chocolate. If it was fourteen, you would've counted fourteen."

Shrugging nonchalantly, she began removing the birds from the duffle, one by one. "I will tell you this. Whatever you niggas doing on these drops, it better tighten up. You and Rex's bags have been short every time one of y'all come to drop off and that shit leaves count fucked up on my end. Now I ain't said shit to Tipton about this because I know we doubling up or whatever, but I'm not slaving over this shit flipping dope for you clowns to be fucking up," she said with seriousness booming through her tone.

"First of all, whatever Tipton gives me is what I give you. Don't even try me on no shit like that. Everybody is on edge about this nigga, Dejuan. So, he's probably messing up his count for being sidetracked with this dummy," Sincere addressed.

"Fuck Dejuan, ain't nobody studding that fool. He around here popping pills like an AIDS patient and smoking all his money out of a weed bong. That should be the last person on Tipton's mind. Maybe if y'all niggas go out a little more. We could be relaxing instead of acting like were apart of Adolf Hitler's meth camp." Chocolate kept her attention on the packaged drugs in front of her.

"Try telling that to him ya damn self. That man is programmed on working 24/8. That's why I have my fun when I hit Miami. He ain't allowing us to get no break time in between all this money-making. I already told everybody before I came on board that I wasn't a slave. So, I'm not sure how long this runner shit gonna ride with me."

Not commenting on the smart remark, she decided to lighten up the conversation, "Y'all niggas are just some wimps. All y'all have to do is speak ya mind. I'll get him to rest for a day to let everyone step out. Maybe it'll ease this fake ass tension you carrying around."

"It ain't never no tension when I'm dealing with anything. I'm moving to build my own moves so quite frankly I don't give a fuck." He moved toward the door with a confident strut like he was the man of the year.

"Don't mix your feelings with business, Sir. Remember that," Chocolate stressed before he walked out.

She picked up her cell to call Tipton. She placed the phone to her ear and began busting down the pure cocaine.

"Waddup?

"I don't mean to interrupt you, but I think we need to have a sit-down."

"What do you mean? What happened?"

"Innovation happened, nigga. Tomorrow morning, we need to discuss things as a whole for this operation. I can fill you in on what's transpiring then."

"Cool, tomorrow it is," Tipton replied before ending the call.

Chocolate stood from the table and moved to secure the front door. Before she could attach the locks, Sincere stepped back inside causing her to jump. "Nigga you scared the shit out of me. Did you forget something?"

His face was blank and unreadable. "Yeah, I just wanted you to know that whatever we speak on is between us."

"Uh, okay. You're saying that because?"

"I'm just letting you know," he threatened indirectly before leaving back out.

Chapter 7

After awaking the next morning, Tipton jumped in the shower and prepared for the meeting that was at hand. Business was moving perfectly, and Sleepy's words were now starting to add up phenomenally. The more he progressed, it allowed his operation to spread wider. Atlanta was only the base. A mere steppingstone to lock down the entire outskirts. Now that he was pushing for different states. He knew different attitudes would appear. When it was money flowing abundantly, everyone was happy. That was an action he expected. But when motherfuckers started to make irrational ass statements. It placed a pause on work until he was sure who was really down for the team. There were no exceptions for anyone. Not even the closest ones.

As he dabbed on a little Gucci Guilty Cologne, Janita opened their bedroom door. "Tipton, everyone is downstairs waiting on you. I'm going to take Kimmi out with me if that's okay?"

He walked over to her and placed a delicate kiss on her forehead. "That's fine baby, but make sure you remember what tonight is. We getting a little alone time, and I'm quite sure Kimmi would want to catch a movie in the family room with us."

"Of course, love, I'll call you when we're on our way back."

After checking himself in the mirror one last time, Tipton headed downstairs to get the show on the road. Rex, Chocolate, Sincere and Halo sat at the kitchen table engaged in their own activities. The new workers were aligned around the walls in deep conversation until the boss man stepped into the room.

Tipton cleared his throat and took a seat at the table.

Chocolate decided to come over earlier and prepare a large breakfast for the crew, so they were all occupied with a plate of her delicious cooking. Smiles were on mostly everyone's face, so it was surely the time to break the news of what this meet up was for.

"If I can have all y'all attention for a second. This will be over within a few minutes," Tipton spoke causing all the small talk to cease.

"I've been pushing to expand our business. Over the past few months, we've had sales that increased beyond the normal heights. Thanks to Chocolate our product has touched every side of this city. The teams that we've place together has been handling business, and that's something I can applaud you all for. I have someone I want you all to meet." Tipton stood to his feet just as the Demon crossed the threshold of the kitchen. "This is my new assistant. His name is Demon. He's here for the protection of this crew, including Halo. Now my point of saying this is because I'm hearing a lot of slick talking going on in the midst of this team. That's some shit I'm not about to tolerate."

Halo removed his pistol, placed one in the chamber and sat it on the table. All he waited for was Tipton to call out the slime one and all problems would disappear with a blink.

"Easy Halo, I'm sure whoever has something to say will be man enough to speak up. How about you guys, anybody got some deep shit on their mind?" Tipton asked while eyeing all the faces in his kitchen.

"What the hell is this truth or dare? Tell us who said what, bro?" Rex said with agitation in his tone.

"Shut the fuck up nigga. You would know if this had anything to do with you." Tipton smirked.

"Smooth." Rex lit up his blunt of weed.

"As I was saying. Does anyone have a problem with how

shit is being run? Is there anyone who wants to take their check and disperse to do your own thing? If it is, you better speak now or forever hold your peace," Tipton spat while cutting his eyes over to Sincere

The silence that filled the air was sharper than a butcher knife. Everyone expected a gun to erupt, but it ended with Tipton taking his seat. "This is the last type of meeting I want to have like this. There should never be a day where I feel anybody by my side is thinking crazy. You kill the seed before it even gets a chance to grow. Even if its someone who you care for dearly. I would expect you all to do the same to me."

"Well, since that is cleared can we please jump back to this product? I have thirty-four keys that need to be distributed and this shit ain't gonna sell itself," Chocolate broke the thick tension.

"Of course." Tipton smiled. "Business is always a pleasure. Now we need to think about what's at hand y'all. In the next few months, I'm going to start spreading us out. New York, Texas, maybe even Detroit. I got it in the process so all we gotta do is bump this shit. stack it and expand. Is everybody on the same page?"

"Hell yeah, we on the same page. Now can we please roll up some more bud and cut a fan on in this hot ass kitchen." Rex wiped the small amount of sweat from his forehead.

Laughing, Tipton nodded. "Facts, if all is well y'all can proceed with your daily activities. Tonight is payday so after you shut shop down. We all pulling back up to the headquarters to divide this pie."

After everyone grabbed a small bag of reup. They began to disperse one by one. As Sincere stood to leave, Tipton followed him to the front door.

"Sincere?"

"Wassup?" He wore a fake smile trying to hide his anger.

"You a'ight, my nigga? You seem upset about something?"

Before he could respond, Halo walked into the living room gun in hand. Their eyes met for a slight second and he could tell his energy was being sensed. "Of course, my brother, I'm just feeling a little sick man. I think it was some shit that I ate last night or something. I'm good," he lied.

"Say less, make sure you're on time tonight." Tipton placed a light punch on his shoulder."

"Sure thing, bro."

He left out of the crib with a mug instantly plastered back on his face. No one was in control of how he moved or talked. A nigga was grown, and damn sure wasn't into being tried like a teenager who needed to be put on. Now that it was clear that Chocolate was a rat for Tipton. His new steps were gonna be calculated to perfection. If a motherfucker was still worried about his lane after that. The indirect threats would be taken personally.

****

Three Weeks Later

Tipton and Janita's wedding reception was beyond beautiful. From their attire down to the decorations sparkled throughout the entire event. The choice of classic black tuxedoes was Tipton's idea. Every male that stepped through the door was smelling great and draped in some of the best designer suits. From the elderly men of Janita's family, down to Tipton's personal friends.

Janita, on the other hand, chose the color grey for the women. It was soothing and mellowed the mood for the amazing wedding. Her gorgeous grey, silk gown was hugging her healthy frame and the cute Chinese puffballs in her hair complimented her magnificent smile. The makeup she wore was applied with perfection, and every second the music pumped through the speaker. She moved around grooving with the family.

After sharing their first dance of the night. Tipton whispered in her ear, "I'm so proud to be your husband."

Blushing with a bright smirk, she kissed his lips. "Uh-huh, what you up to?"

"Nothing, I'm just admiring this wonderful picture right now. You look so beautiful today, and this was a moment that I've been waiting for since I met you. I'm happy!"

Twirling her fingers through his chin hair, she pecked his lips." I should be the one that's happy. You made my dream come true and I will never forget this day. You're my king, and I'm grateful to have a man of your caliber to call my husband."

Before Tipton could reply, his attention followed the loud voice that ranged out in his ceremony. "What the fuck going on in this bitch? You mean to tell me I wasn't invited!" Dejuan shouted with Peaches on his arm.

"Baby, stay here?" Tipton ordered as he drifted from her side.

"Look Juan they got wings and everything in this motherfucker!" Peaches yelled while fixing her a small plate.

Halo spotted Tipton moving towards them and quickly followed. Before Dejuan could get another word out, he was cornered off.

"You must really got a death wish, nigga? This is the wrong place to try this stupid shit boy." Tipton's jaws clenched in anger.

Halo stood behind him clutching the pistol that rested on his waist. The entire wedding was like it paused and everyone's attention was now on the two men who stood face to face.

"What, how could you not invite me to this big day of yours? Last time I checked we were boys, nigga. What type of way is that to treat your best friend?"

"Were not fucking friends, idiot. In case you don't know I have a ticket out on your head so big that God is gonna turn your ass in for the money. I suggest you leave and catch me at a different time. Cause this isn't it." Tipton tried to humble himself.

Just when he figured things couldn't get any worse. Peaches stepped from the small crowd. "Nigga you around here getting married and shit when you were just telling me you wanna come back home. Your daughter is struggling and you around this bitch living it up."

Eyeing her with hatred, he could tell Peaches was surely on something. Her body was deformed horribly. Her ass was gone, and her titties were sinking like a dirty ship. The bags under her eyes said she wasn't the same woman he met at Chocolate's party six years back.

"Peaches, you're pathetic. You're a poor excuse for a mother and you don't know how deep you're digging yourself into a hole. I'm asking you to leave."

"Just give me the word, God." Halo's face balled with anger."

Holding up a hand, Tipton tried to ease his friend's nerves. Janita swerved from behind him, pointing a stern finger. "Tipton, who the hell is this?"

"It's my child's mother, I'll handle it, baby." He grabbed her waist.

"No! That's the bitch who came into my shop the night it was burned down. That's your baby mama?" She mugged.

"Yeah, hoe, that's me. How did all your paintings turn out,

medium rare or crispy?"

Tipton quickly snatched Janita back as she tried to jump for Peaches' neck. "Baby please, just let me handle it. Don't mess up your day for these people."

Sending a hard slap to his right cheek, Janita shouted causing the music to cease. "How could you sit here and stop me after what she did? This bitch destroyed my dream and you standing right here talking to her like y'all the best of friends. She took my passion away from me, Tipton."

"Baby girl, is everything okay?" Janita's father asked with a confused face.

"Yes, Sir, it's just a misunderstanding."

"Fix this, Tipton. This is not a good impression for the family son," he replied grabbing Janita to walk her back over toward the family.

Turning his attention to Dejuan and Peaches. Tipton grabbed the bridge of his nose." I tried to bare patience with y'all but I see it's being taken for granted. Both of y'all junkie ass motherfuckers got ten seconds to get the fuck outta here before I have you escorted out!"

"Nigga I'm here for my money, bro. Ever since you did that bid I ain't seen a coin of all that shit I worked hard to run up for you. You treat Rex like he the true hustler. He the one fucked the paper up. Everybody knows that you a drug dealer, Tip. You run around here acting like you a businessman. That's a lie," Dejuan spat.

"What do you want, Juan? Regardless of how you feel, you're gonna leave here empty-handed."

Placing his hand on Tipton's shoulder was the last action he took before Halo collided a fist into his jaw knocking him unconscious. Halo grabbed him by the collar, snatched Peaches by her dry ass weave and drug them both towards the exit.

"Get the fuck off me bitch ass nigga! Tipton, you're gonna die for this shit. I promise that." Peaches kicked as Halo jerked her head violently.

Staring at the catastrophe unfold in front of him. Tipton shook his head. All Janita's family were looking in amazement and the entire night was ruined because his wife was sitting in the corner spilling a bucket of tears. The wonderful day he planned for months was going down the drain, and it was one he surely wouldn't hear the last of.

"Are you in need of my assistance, Sir?" Demon asked with a calm expression.

"Nah, he ain't in need of nothing, right now. Just give us a second if you don't mind, Hannibal," Rex said before stepping in front of Tipton."

"I don't have time for any jokes right now, Rex. I'm not in the mood."

"Me either, this clown ass bozo just barged his way into your wedding and violated. Look around, bro, its nothing but family and friends here."

"What's that supposed to mean?"

"That means how in the fuck did this man find us. We're in a private rented building that has a security team sitting right out front. Did this nigga sleep in your trunk or what?"

"No dumbass, Janita posted the wedding event on social media. It's quite obvious. Not to mention this hungry ass hoe Peaches. They were too comfortable strolling up through this bitch. He knew I wasn't gonna touch him in front of all those people," Tipton responded while straightening the wrinkles from his suit.

A few guests were still quiet as if they were waiting on a different outcome. The ecstatic wedding that was just in effect was officially fading down, and Halo's reaction with Dejuan obviously had everybody on thin edges. Some things were easy to spiral out of control. This was just a night he couldn't contain.

"So, what the fuck are you gonna do? You let this fool storm all in yo' girl shit. It's like that boy ass itching for death." Rex folded his arms.

"What I'm gonna do is finish my event for my wife. Then I'm going home. The night is young, and I refuse to see this end for Janita from the cause of Dejuan's bitch ass. He's signed his own contract."

"Smooth." Rex smiled before venturing off back into the crowd.

"Let the party continue people!" Tipton yelled out as if all was normal.

Within seconds, the music was back bumping and smiles were starting to glow back up. That was all he needed to see before he spotted Janita sitting alone.

Chris Green

Chapter 8

As Tipton pulled the car into the driveway of his home and parked, Janita climbed out of the passenger seat slamming the door behind her.

Tipton exhaled, removed the keys from the ignition and headed inside. After the wedding reception was back on track, Janita still took the initiative to ignore him for the rest of the night. The sweet gestures he made were unaccepted. Even the dance he tried to share was denied. It was hard to see the woman who tore down your vision stand in your face as if your passion was worth nothing. She had a reason to be mad in Tipton's head, but the moment she heard about Peaches being his child's mother sent the wave crashing drastically back down.

He stepped into their bedroom and watched as she took off her gown. Her stiff movements indicated that she was still beyond hot. Instead of arguing, Tipton wanted to comfort. To ease the tension from the woman he promised to love and cherish. It was hard to break a woman's pain with affection, but tonight there was no other choice.

Stripping out of all his clothes, he removed his boxers letting them drop to the floor. Then walked behind her, wrapped his arms around her waist and slid his tongue across her neck.

A small jolt shot through Janita's legs causing her to turn around, viewing Tipton's naked body. She turned her head from the hypnotizing teaser. His muscular arms did the work by pulling her closer. His hands gripped her ass firmly and she could still smell his Polo Blue cologne he put on this morning before they departed from the house.

"Nah, I don't think I'm in the mood for all that Tipton." She tried to push him off.

He reached his fingers underneath her slip and twirled her clit in one swift motion.

"Nooo!" she whined with her back arching lightly.

"Janita, I'm your husband now. You really gonna deny me on the night of our wedding," he whispered before pulling off her bra.

Her eyes were closed, pants from her lips could be lightly heard as he followed with dropping her panties.

"You don't deserve it."

"But you do," he mumbled before taking one of her breasts into his mouth, gently sucking on her nipple.

He placed three wet delicate kisses and performed the same affection to the other. Sliding two fingers down her tummy, he trailed them past her belly button until he reached Janita's plump womanhood. He pinched her love button a few times. She threw her head back in satisfaction

"Stoooppp!"

Ignoring her fake pleas, he picked her up into his arms and walked her over to the bed and eased her down. Tipton stroked his erection before sliding it up and down her slippery slit. All Janita could do was pout as he began to slide deeply inside her. The feeling was so good, her legs quaked once he reached the bottom. The bliss sent butterflies fluttering through her stomach. Before she could release a moan, he dipped lightly inside her.

"Daddyyy!" her lips muttered before she shook lightly.

"I got you, baby. I know today was hard for you. Just enjoy your moment," he said before smoothly sliding in her walls harder.

As her kitty began to glisten, Tipton locked in his rhythm. His strokes were deeper and longer. The sound of her juices quaked as if the kitty box was on the loudspeaker. All he wanted to do was be delicate. To calmly fill her pussy until she gave him every drop of that passion juice.

"Oooohhh shit!" Janita jumped as Tipton began to have his way.

He gripped her waist and pounded with precision until she began to claw at his back.

"I'm sorry, baby," he grunted before easing off her.

He turned her over softly on all fours. Her bubble behind wobbled. Her skin complexion enticed the beautiful color of her eyes as she stared across her shoulder at him. Tipton positioned himself behind Janita's apple and entered her slowly.

"Mmm!"

"Just relax, baby."

Spreading her ass, he guided his dick between her cheeks. Tonight, was about positive energy. It was about love. To build the walls of a home and stamp that the marriage was going to be forever. It was time to exploit everything Janita had to offer. Her emotions were intertwining with every stroke Tipton made. The entire night was about to be pleasing and soothing. Calm enough to make her kitty flow like a silent river on a full moon night. It was magical. The true first time he made love with someone that he would adore and cherish forever.

****

Awaking from his sleep, Tipton's eyes landed on Janita. Her head was pressed against his chest and her warm body was latched on to him tighter than a koala bear in a tree. She looked so beautiful, even while sleep. Her light snores caused her lips to pucker lightly as if she was blowing him a kiss. She was truly a trophy.

Easing her down on the bed, she rolled lightly over and

continued her beauty rest. Tipton rose to his feet and stretched before making his way downstairs. He passed by Halo's room. He could see that his friend was still burned out from all the wedding chaos. After the reception, Tipton sent him out to have a little fun with Sonya before he returned home. It was never good to bring negative energy into the comfort zone of your own home. Judging from the way the two was snuggled in the bed said that they weren't being too friendly in the sheets last night either.

Smirking, Tipton continued down to the living room and headed for the kitchen, then paused. He stared at the woman who snooped around his front yard.

"What the fuck?" he mumbled to himself.

He opened the front door and stepped outside to meet Detective Sandra Elliot eyeing the cars aligned inside his garage.

"Uh, excuse me? What the hell are you doing on my property?"

She cleared her throat and took a step forward. "Good morning, Mr. White. I'm sure you wanna know what the hell I'm doing in your front lawn at eight-thirty in the morning? I just wanna let you know before you start cussing and flipping out that it's damn sure for a good reason."

"Do tell." Tipton mugged before crossing his arms.

"Well, for starters, I've been doing a little background check on you. You're very successful for a young man that just left a prison cell. I guess you were selling all the Debbie pies through the system in order to get that hundred and fifty thousand dollars building down by Peachtree?"

Hearing her remark, he smiled. "Yeah, that took years to save. Lots of hard work and dedication. I'm glad every black man isn't a slave, it feels good."

"Ain't that the truth," she replied sarcastically.

"Yeah, it is."

Sensing that he was about to take the conversation elsewhere, she decided to be brief. "Of course, you know I'm still over the case about Lisa? Forensics are back and we have something that's tying a suspect to the crime. This is the reason I'm here. It's been brought to my attention that the lamp was holding a set of fingerprints. The same weapon that was used to kill this woman was used by someone close. Closer than your jugular vein, Mr. White. My job is to offer chances. Valuable ones that could clear you away from this so your aunt can rest easily. Don't you want that?"

"Unfortunately my aunt has been dead for months. Her soul would never be able to rest because you have obnoxious and delirious people like you who want to blame everybody but yourself. Instead of you doing your dirty ass job. You wanna come play questions and answers because you don't know shit, and y'all never do. If you had information on my aunt, why aren't you making any arrests? All it seems like a whole bunch of harassing. I'ma tell you like this because I'm starting to lose my patience with you, old lady. If you trespass on my property or bother me again. I'll have you arrested and pressed by my lawyer team for a full investigation. My lawyers are great. So, good that they can turn your detective badge into an ID card working as a cashier at the Six Flags amusement park."

She placed both hands behind her back and made sure her holstered gun was shown before forcing a light chuckle. "Mr. White, I don't take threats lightly. I'll leave you with this. Your aunt's murderer is so close to you that these prints could damn near be your own. I smell bullshit every time my eyes catch a small glimpse of you. Your disrespectful posture spells trouble and I know you're hiding some-thing. Unlike most I'm not scared of you, lawyers or treacherous little killers. Be aware, Mr. White." She turned around to make her way down his driveway.

He watched her climb inside the police cruiser to leave. He headed back inside to find Halo posted at the front door with his gun in hand. "Everything okay, God?"

"Yeah, this Matlock looking ass detective keep following me around like I'm a suspect or some shit. This bitch just won't stop. I can see the look in her eyes that it's something deeper," Tipton spoke before walking into the kitchen.

"Maybe she's trying to pin the murder on you, God. You can never trust any cops. It's in their natural instinct to blame the wrong person. Whether innocent or guilty."

"Tell me about it. Ever since I met this bitch, I been having the chills when she comes around. It's like a prison bid waiting to happen when I see her dumb ass face. I don't even know how the fuck she found my house. I been investing in a few new things so we can relocate soon. I just don't know how I'm gonna move all this money."

"Easy overseas, God. You playing with too much dough now. Better to go ahead and place things in effect before it's too late. This woman seems very interested in you."

"I know, playing around she'll make me get her ass brushed," Tipton said seriously.

"You want me to handle her?" Halo raised an eyebrow.

"Nah, we will give her just enough room to breathe a little. If she keeps fooling around with the fuckery I want, you to shoot her ass twenty times."

"Whatever you say, God."

Tipton stood to his feet. "The new guns that we bought. Do you think it's enough to build you a four-man team along with Demon?"

"God, you got enough guns to take down three banks at one time. I'm sure I can handle that."

"Good, we about to shift this shit up a little. I need you to ride with me somewhere later on after I pick up, Kimmi. If shit slides the right way after I talk to, Logan. We will be hustling in two different states at the end of the month. What you think about doing a little business in Omaha for a few weeks?" Tipton asked with a curious expression. "All you gotta do is set up shop with a few of our workers. Lay down the law, once you see to it that shit is in our palms. You can come back."

A wicked smile spread across Halo's face. "Of course, God, that's a pleasure."

Chris Green

Chapter 9

Sincere breezed past the highway sign on the expressway and pulled off the exit of Miami Florida. His dark tints on the rented Black Tahoe hid his identity as he made his way toward Kenny Quick's penthouse suite. The time was passing by briefly over the past few weeks. After the first few drops. Sincere was nervous to travel back and forth with a large amount of weight. Kenny's words of encouragement were a major factor in his new relaxed image.

After all, he practically ran Miami with his flamboyant speech and amazing hustle game. Kenny was the Lebron James to his city. He conquered without being taken through the slumps. If it was time to talk his way off the product. You would be purchasing the entire shipment after his mouth finally closed. It was perfect for the numbers Tipton needed moved.

After showing Sincere that he could make an extra paper flow. He began to stick around Kenny more. It started to become his weekly routine. The extra twenty grand equaled to nearly a hundred thousand every month. It was a mission for money and if he kept it moving just right. He was gonna pass Tipton's small business and go into shop for himself.

Twenty minutes had passed before he pulled inside the building's entrance. The sweet smell of the Miami fast life touched his nose when he parked and stepped out of the car. It was wonderful, a vacation to get some pussy and make the easy bread was the reason he continued to indulge in Kenny's activities. He removed the bags from the backseat, made his way through the entrance and headed straight for the top floor. After exiting the elevator, he trailed down the hallway until he reached the security guard who posted outside the presidential room.

"Sincere, good to see ya. Kenny's waiting for you." He opened the door and stepped to the side.

"Cool," he replied before walking in.

The smell of exotic weed was in the air and Kenny's mind was wrapped in a heated phone call.

"Listen to me motherfucker. My name ain't Quick for nothing. You either have the loot by tonight, or I'll get rid of your entire little team by morning. If it's not about the money, chew on my fucking nuts!" He yelled before hanging up the cell.

He tossed it on the glass table, looked up into Sincere's eyes and smiled. "I had a feeling you would he popping around here soon. I've planned the most terrific night for us, my friend."

"Oh, really, and what would that consist of?" He sat the bags at Kenny's feet.

As he jumped from the couch, he snickered like a greedy criminal waiting to steal a ten-foot safe. He walked to his master bedroom and opened the door. "Ladies, can you help me out here?" he spoke with authority.

Within a blink of the eye, six women strutted smoothly out into the front room. All their skin tones and race were different. The sight of their intoxicating lingerie sent a slight sensation through his manhood.

"Who are these ladies?" Sincere smirked as he eyed all the women with lust.

"These are my minions." Kenny chuckled. "They're gonna be at the new strip joint I'm about to open at the end of the year. I need you to have a little fun and see who's the best if you know what I mean."

"Really, why do I deserve such a good gift?" he questioned before walking over to stand between the girls.

"What type of question is that? Without you, I would be

dry on my ass. You saved Miami with your coca, my friend. It was an opportunity to progress and you wasted no time showing me how loyal you truly were. Tonight, we're gonna have a little fun. I'm gonna take you to a club and introduce you to one of the most important individuals of this operation. They've been dying to meet you," Kenny said before grabbing him a fresh bottle of Caviar.

"That sounds great, but why do they wanna meet me. I'm good with handling business with you."

Well, of course, but that's not where it ends, Sincere. You've stamped your product on my turf and I'm afraid these big customers wanna deal with you personally. I encourage you to expand with me. This isn't the ordinary buyer. We're talking about numbers that double over mines within a few weeks. I'm talking about millions, Sincere."

As he watched the gorgeous black woman rub against his chest. He grabbed the ass of a white woman who licked her tongue repeatedly across his earlobe. The women were swarming him slowly but aggressively. "I hear you, Kenny. As long as you vouch for them, I'm with it."

"Good, now have you some fun. I need a little rest, so I'll leave you to attend to the dolls however long you choose."

Flashing a devilish smile, he gazed at all the mesmerizing ladies. "You mean I get to taste all of them?"

"All the tasting you can handle, my friend. That's what this game is all about, satisfaction," Kenny replied before leaving the room.

As he stood, staring at the women in silence. A slim Spanish female reached for his zipper.

****

The night was starting to grow old and Janita knew that

Tipton would surely be home within the next hour or so. The love was booming in the air and it surely wasn't that mystery love affection. He was everything and more. The steamy passion he placed in her bones was like a trigger to his touch. He knocked down the arrogant walls and placed the submissive freaky housewife into her spirit. It felt like heaven.

She stepped out of the shower, headed into the room and started lotioning her body. The new sweet foundation of peace was at its all-time high, and if all grew to be perfected. A beautiful baby would be placed in her vision.

Boom!

The loud crashing sound under Janita's feet caused her to jump up in fear. She stood still for a slight second, then it happened again.

Boom!

She quickly reached for her TV remote to view the house camera. After repeatedly pressing the button, she watched as one out of three men caved their small garage door in with a violent kick.

Boom!

Panicking, she grabbed her phone before rushing into the large walk-in closet.

****

Holding his gun in front of him, Dejuan stood in the middle of Tipton's living room. The two shooters with him wasted no time trashing the bottom level of the house for valuables or money. After the incident with the wedding. Dejuan made it his business to confront the blue-eyed tough guy personally. There was only one way to make a nigga respect you and it surely wasn't gonna come by knocking him out in the midst of a marriage event.

"Rip this bitch up. Whatever we find, we split. I'll go check upstairs while y'all search down here," Dejuan spat before making his way to the top floor.

Aiming his pistol with caution, he opened the first room. Flicking on the light switch, he glared at the simple set up. One flat screen, a bed, a dresser, it was obviously not the master bedroom. Quickly searching the closet, he found nothing. He started pulling the dresser draws out and received the same results, nothing.

After heading out, he closed the door behind him and proceeded across the hall. He stepped inside Tipton's room. He could smell the sweet scent of Janita's Mango peach lotion looming in the air. He moved over to the bed and picked up the damp towel that was sitting next to the strong scented bottle. Then he paused as if a pair of eyes was on his back and began looking around the large room.

****

"Nine-one-one!" the operator spoke through the phone just as Dejuan stepped foot through their bedroom door. Janita was trembling with fear, her hands shook gently as she tried to whisper in the phone.

"Someone is in my home."

"Ma'am, did you say someone was in your home? What are they doing?"

"I don't know, three men are in my house and I'm in the closet," she said before placing a hand over her mouth. The sight of Dejuan picking up the towel sent chills down her spine. He was literally a few feet away from her and there was absolutely no way for her to fight off three men and make it down to the front door. The pace of her heartbeat increasing forced a light whimper to escape from between her lips.

Watching Dejuan's eyes zoom in on the closet, she panicked. His body turned towards her direction, and his feet began to move on a mission. Before he could reach the door. A loud security alarm began to ring alerting that the authorities were on the way.

Shifting his feet nervously, Dejuan jerked his head around to see where the computerized voice was flowing from. Without wasting any more time, he fled from the room and rushed back downstairs.

"Let's get the fuck out of here. The cops about to flood this shit!" He shouted before exiting the same way he came in, but not without grabbing a few miscellaneous things.

The two thugs swiftly followed behind and departed from the home.

Janita peeped out of the closet and fumbled to unlock her cellphone, then she dialed Tipton's number. She glanced at the camera on her screen. Things grew quiet in the home and her eyes couldn't spot any movement on the television.

"Waddup, baby, I was just thinking about you," he spoke through the line.

"Tipton, come home now!" Janita cried

"What's wrong?"

"The guy from the wedding, he broke in the house, and he wasn't alone. I'm scared!"

"Halo, turn the car around!" Tipton yelled. "Janita, are they still in the house?"

"I don't think so, I'm still in the closet upstairs. Tipton, please hurry."

Baby, I'm coming right now. I need you to stay calm and listen to me. I want you to look on the closet shelf. The black shoebox that's sitting under that Gucci bag. Do you see it?" he asked calmly.

"Yes." A bead of sweat rushed down her forehead as she

pulled it down.

"Open it up, it's a gun inside it. Janita be careful, it's a bullet in the chamber. If anyone opens that closet door, shoot. Don't come out no matter what you hear. Do you understand?" Tipton asked.

"Yes."

"I'll be there in fifteen minutes," he replied before ending the call.

"What is it, God?"

"That fuck boy just popped the knob in his brain. He broke into the house. Hurry up and get us there." Tipton bit on his bottom lip before removing his pistol.

Playtime for Juan was up. The concealed feelings for his disrespectful actions were finally at the max with Tipton, and there was no other decision. He had to be removed.

****

As Halo swerved the car inside the driveway. Tipton jumped out before it could come to a complete stop. His gun was in hand aiming for anything strange. Noticing the garage door was caved in. He moved quickly through the area and entered the house. The bottom part of the home was completely destroyed. His heart fluttered with worry causing him to yell her name.

"Janita!"

He ran up the stairs, entered their room and headed straight for the closet. Tipton opened the small door and found Janita sitting in the corner with a face full of tears. He kneeled beside her. "Baby, are you okay?"

"Tipton, he was in our home. Why is this happening to us?" she asked with a confused face.

"I know ma, don't worry. It's gonna be okay. I want you

Chris Green

to get your things packed so we can leave, okay," he mumbled before placing a kiss on her forehead.

Tipton helped Janita to her feet, then glanced at Halo who stood to the side quietly. "Bro, I need to get everybody on one accord. Call, Chocolate, tell her to go pick up Kimmi and slide over here. I'm moving tomorrow."

"I'm on it, God," he replied before pulling out his cell.

Tipton grabbed the spare key to his safe, he rushed into the closet and began clearing out all his money. Janita stood behind him with a worried look.

"Tipton?"

"Yeah?"

"Why don't you just stop, I'm here for you with money or without it. This man is trying to ruin you and nothing good could come from an evil person like him. You can just quit before someone gets hurt," she spoke with worry.

After stuffing the last of the cash into his duffle. He stood face to face with her. "I understand you're scared, baby. No matter how bad things might look I just want you to know that I have things under control."

"Tipton, that man didn't come to rob us. He came to kill. It's like he knew I was here alone. He looked directly at the closet. He could've had me if it wasn't for the alarm going off. I've never been that scared in my life," Janita explained. She wiped her tears as he lifted her chin.

"Listen, I would never let anyone hurt you, Nita. You're my Queen and I'm not putting you at risk. I'm gonna handle that boy. He's never gonna be able to break in another house for the rest of his life. As far as stopping, I can't do that right now. There's too many people who depend on me to eat."

"What about them feeding themselves? You can't help everyone win, Tipton."

"Understood, but I made a vow to help them until they

reach a point where my assistance is no longer needed. This isn't forever, Janita. It's only until we all make enough to leave this shit alone for good. Just pack your things. We will be in another house by morning," he replied before heading deeper into the closet.

He removed a small wooden floorboard, dug inside and continued to fill different bags full of cash. The last thing he removed was a small arsenal of weapons, clips, and bullets. He stuffed them inside his large tote and placed everything in the center of his bed.

In order to have peace, you must have war. In order to get respect, you must enforce it. Weakness was something Tipton refused to show.

"I did what you said, God. What's next?" Halo asked anticipating a little gunplay.

"We meet up and sit down with everyone. I'm gonna switch a few things up. He touched my family. Now I'ma touch his."

"Whatever you say, God."

****

Eight Hours Later: 6:35 a.m.

Chocolate stepped out of her new white Lincoln Continental, pulling her brown peak coat closed. Her hair was pulled back into a ponytail, and the new French manicure on her fingers was an extra highlight to her. magnificent appearance. It was strange to hear that Tipton was calling a random meeting. Especially when it wasn't at the crib. It was something new which obviously meant there was a problem.

She walked across the large parking lot and entered the small brick gym. The inside of the building was warmer than she expected. Tipton, Halo, and Rex sat in a small circle of chairs engaged in a conversation. Along with Demon and the young shooters who were aligned against the boxing ring and walls.

Everyone's head shifted to Chocolate as she entered the room. "Is there a reason why we're meeting up at this sweaty ass gym?"

"Yeah, there is. From now own the only people who are gonna know where I live is my day ones. Dejuan broke into my house last night while Janita was home by herself," Tipton answered before pulling on the rolled marijuana.

"He did what!"

"Goddamn, Chocolate, I think we all heard that clearly. Can you lower your tone," Rex spat with an irritated tone.

"Fuck you, nigga, I'm talking to Tipton. Did you say this nigga broke into your house?" she repeated with her hands balled up.

"Yeah, he did, but that's gonna be handled. I've given Dejuan chance after chance to let us be. It was only for the sake of him being a brother to me. I never chose to hurt him because it's no different than me hurting one of you guys. That feeling doesn't live in me no more. It's just business, he violated and the only way to redeem himself is putting a gun to his temple and pulling the trigger."

"So, what are we supposed to do from here? We have no way to be safe if this nigga knows where you stay. He probably got the drop on all our spots. That bitch is sneaky, Tipton, you know that" Rex questioned.

"We expand, I have three different teams which is you, Chocolate, and Halo. Once I find out where the next three targeted states are. We're taking our different crew and relocating. The mission is to set up shop in your selected area and enforce the ruling on whoever's so-called in charge. I want you to take the new teams. Kill the workers if necessary and explain to them the new prices and the way our product moves. If the leader is rebellious, kill them and take the turf forcefully. I've searched around for the past three months and these are some of the most ruthless niggas I could find that's standing around y'all, right now. If we move correctly it will all fall perfectly.

"When are we supposed to be doing this?" Chocolate butted in.

"In due time, for now, we're gonna move bricks only. No breakdown, use the few connections we have, and the rest will fall in place. We're not hurting for money so don't press to make it."

"And what about, Dejuan?" Chocolate asked. Just the taste of his name made her want to puke. He was the bottom crab of the barrel. An itch that wouldn't stop until you scratched his brain with a few bullets.

"Don't worry, I'm sure he'll pop up after he finds the little surprise Demon left for him."

The buzzing of Tipton's phone paused his next remark. He reached into his pocket, removed it and found a text from Rika.

"Your assistance is needed."

He stood to his feet, tapping Halo's shoulder. "It's time to ride."

"Hold up, you ain't even explained what's next, Tipton. You moving around all cool and shit like Mr. Rogers in the neighborhood. What are we supposed to do about this man running around all crazy?" Chocolate said with hostility in her tone.

"Calm down, the main mission is for me to make sure your safe, right? In order for me to do that, you have to sit back and let me run the show, Chocolate. As I said, you're about to prepare for another state of your own and it's gonna be easy. I even got someone who's gonna ride with you." Tipton smiled.

Chocolate folded her arms, gazing at him curiously. "Who? I hope you don't think I'm going anywhere with Mr. long leg over there." She pointed at Rex. "Neither am I doing anything with, Sincere."

"You mean Granddaddy long leg little girl." Rex chuckled."

"Vienna motherfucker."

"Both of y'all stop it, I'm not sending y'all nowhere together so that should be the last thing on your mind. Just know that my plug has put some things together for us and it's gonna be easy if we fly out. Handle the business and come back. Tomorrow, we will meet up and discuss how many men are moving out without y'all. So, I suggest you pick some niggas that ain't ready to come back home so fast," Tipton replied before walking out of the boxing gym with Halo behind him.

Chapter 10

After arriving at their destination, Tipton made his way into Sleepy's home with Halo by his side. The introduction from the butler was the usual causing Sleepy to walk over and greet him with a firm handshake.

"Tipton, I'm glad that you could make it."

"My pleasure," he replied while looking at the two men and woman who sat at the table quietly.

"I would like to introduce you to a few of my friends. This is Milo from Nebraska," Sleepy announced.

Halo looked at the man with a stupid grin before flashing a smile.

"The lovely woman sitting on the right is, Kima. She's a head honcho out in Cali."

"Hey, Tipton!" She flirted with a sexy smirk.

"Waddup."

"And this is, Biggs. He's been a loyal person in my corner for years. Georgia has been his stomping ground, and he knows how to market something if it needs to be pushed."

"Wassup, Young Blood," he greeted with a head nod."

"Now the reason I bring you here on such short notice is because I want them to have an understanding on who they're about to be dealing with. The game is twisted in many ways, and nothing can be constructed the same without having a flaw, unless it's constructed by the same person," Sleepy said as he took his seat.

"That's true, but how does it apply to all of us?" Tipton asked before placing his back on the wall.

"Simple, it gives you all a chance to come down with an understanding. There's nothing worse in this business than dirty dealings. We're all here because we know how to handle the business. After your skills touch these different states. It will allow you to see the true potential of your hustle. It's a plus for all y'all. That's the reason I called y'all here. Now would be the time to agreed and disagree."

"First of all, Cali is sweet I don't need no hello hustling, but we don't have anything, but some stepped on ass work. I'm too much of a boss bitch to continue serving anyone with this weak ass baking soda drugs," he said that you can help me change that. If it is true then I'm in," Kima spoke before crossing her legs.

"I can do whatever you need as long as we chopping up some funds," Tipton replied with assurance.

"Then you got a deal with me, baby boy, I'm in." She smiled looking him up and down.

"Great. What about you, Milo?" Sleepy asked.

Turning his grey eagle snapback backward. He flashed his six platinum teeth. "It sounds good or whatnot, but we got good dope. So, what's in it for us?"

"Tipton's work is more pure there's a difference," Sleepy replied.

"As I said, that sounds very good. What else?" he countered arrogantly.

"I can guarantee you, I'll make three times your quota in a month's time span. My team is filled with hustlers. Very talented hustlers who can bring it back harder than a D.J. spinning a single. More money would be your answer." Tipton looked him in the eyes with a straight face.

Milo folded his arms and leaned back in his chair. "You a very strong individual to have faith in some shit like that. I'll take your word for it, but even that can be questioned. I'm with it, only if Sleepy gives me a second agreement that whatever goes wrong falls on him."

"Take it however you choose," Sleepy spoke with a calm tone.

"Cool, I'm in then."

Sleepy turned his head to his close associate, Sleepy smiled. "Biggs, what will it be? Can we do business?"

The man chuckled, leaned forward and fired up a black and mild cigar. "No offense, but I've never met this cat in my life."

"Cat ain't my name big man." Tipton stood off the wall.

"Well, Tipton, I've never met you a day in my life. My business is with Sleepy, and Sleepy only. I have money, I have great sales. I need more product. There's nothing you can help me with. As I said, I mean no disrespect," he said before inhaling his cigar again.

"Good," Tipton replied with a phony smile.

Sensing the disagreement going totally wrong, Sleepy interfered. "Understood, but unfortunately there will be no more movement if it's not going through him. My business is now stepping over to his hands. If that'll be a problem I'm sure you will find another plug."

"Of course," Biggs replied arrogantly.

Standing to his feet, Sleepy put his hands together." I thank you all for coming and we will surely be in touch. You're all free to leave."

After watching the small group rise from the table, the butler escorted them to the front door. Tipton and Halo remained and watched as Sleepy fixed himself a small glass of White Remy. He placed the top on his bottle, then walked over to them both. "I think this is gonna go great."

"What makes you say that? I was never aware that this was gonna be a connection meeting. You don't usually hear disagreements when it comes to business," Tipton said with a straight face.

"It's just business, people never come to an agreement hearing things they want. It's always a bargain. Nothing comes free and sometimes you have to bless in order to gain people's interest. I've learned to know there's plenty more who are willing to be in a position that another refuses to play. You are the beast of this operation. Your word is last. The table is set, son. All you have to do is serve." Sleepy looked him the eyes.

Smiling, Tipton nodded. "Son has a nice ring to it. I'm hearing you loud and clear for sure. Maybe it's in the bloodline somewhere." Tipton held out his hand.

Shaking it firmly, Sleepy smirked. "You are this bloodline."

****

Watching the light afternoon fade around the sky, Dejuan drove in his all-black charger. His mind was wrapped around his payday that he knew was coming very soon. His heart was grieving for numerous reasons, but all were meant to happen if God made it that way. It was no turning back from being a loner, to rise all the way alone.

He pulled inside his mother's home, parked his car behind the crib and stepped out. He could smell the dog shit that lingered in the air. He tooted his nose and continued inside. As he stepped through the threshold of her home, Dejuan's heart sank to the bottom of his stomach. His eyes wanted to shed a million teas at once, but his mind couldn't process what he was visualizing. He walked over to his little sister, staring at the large bullet hole in the center of her head.

"Deseray?" he cried lightly placing a hand on her heart. "Deserayyy!" he screamed to the top of his lungs.

He cut his eyes to the living room. His mother's body was sprawled out on the hardwood floor. He ran over to her and dropped to her side. "Mama!" As he viewed her body, he found no gunshot wounds, but her movements were unresponsive. "Oh, my God! Please, mama, wake up." Drool began to slide from the bottom of his mouth.

The vibration of his cellphone caused him to jump. He struggled to remove it from his pocket. He looked at the private number and answered quickly. "Hello?" The tears continued to run down his face.

"Do you see my message now, bro?" Tipton spoke through the line.

Standing to his feet, Dejuan screamed into the phone. "Whyyyyy, you fucking pussy!"

"Calm the fuck down nigga because you know why. Stop yelling like a bitch, so I can say what I need to. I never got a chance to know your sister, so you can see we didn't waste any time on that. On the other note, mama may seem dead, but she ain't. You actually got time to call the ambulance to help her. I watch everything, Dejuan. Like the way you standing in the house with a hand on your forehead."

Hearing the statement caused him to jump and look around the house. He walked over to the blinds. "You hiding and watching me, nigga. Come face me like a man," he spat into the phone receiver.

"Just as I said, I can see everything. Now you only got about thirty minutes before that medicine inside your mama's bloodstream clog up her brain. Then she's gonna die. Walk over to the house phone that's sitting on the brown table and call the ambulance. I'll wait."

It was obvious that Tipton was watching him. He knew that the odds were against him when he was able to call out his movements. His mother was more important, and debating wasn't in the conversation. There was no time to waste. He ran over to the house phone and dialed 911.

"Nine-one-one, this is operator Lisa Woods. What is your

emergency?"

"I found my sister dead and my mother is laying on the floor unconscious. I need an ambulance now!"

"Sir, what is your mother's name, is she breathing?"

"I don't know bitch that's why I said send an ambulance! My address is 1347 West Court Drive, I need help!" he screamed into the phone.

"Sir, the authorities and ambulance are on the way," the dispatcher confirmed.

Dejuan slammed the phone down and placed the cellphone to his ear before kneeling over his mother. "I did what the fuck you said, nigga. Tell me how to help my mama!"

"There is no helping her unless you're a doctor idiot. My advice to you would be to watch your movements. You violated. Wherever I see you, it ends Juan. Please take that and leave this alone," Tipton spat before ending the call.

Hearing the sirens in a near distance, Juan held his mother as the tears fell freely. War was beyond his mind. It was now deeper than anyone could ever feel. Pain quaked through his stomach as he prepared himself to go out harder than Tipton could ever believe. The war would end drastically, and that was a fate everyone wasn't prepared to face.

****

"Look, mama, y'all ain't gotta stress about rent now. I explained that to you earlier, just chill," Chocolate said as she grabbed Kimmi's Burberry coat.

The smell of her mom's house reeked of old ass neck bones and buttermilk cornbread. The dogs were running around hunching everything that moved, and that old ass husband of hers sat on the couch for hours at a time passing gas and changing channels. It was surely time to take Kimmi back to her father were she belonged.

"Girl you know I gotta remind yo' ass about everything. I know my grandbaby probably ain't gonna be back over here for another three months. So, you know I needed to get this little time in," she said before placing a kiss on Kimmi's cheek.

"I know ma, but you know how Tipton is. I should be back soon though."

Just as Chocolate picked up the baby book bag. Peaches stepped through the front door looking like a hooker running from her pimp. Recognizing that her daughter was standing in the living room. She rubbed a hand over her hair to straighten it. "Hey, mommy's babyyy!"

"Mommy!" Kimmi moved over to her in a rush.

Grabbing her, Peaches squeezed with love while raining kisses on her child's forehead. "How are you, pudding?" She squeezed her cheekbone.

"Where have you been? You never come to get me," Kimmi mumbled.

"I know, mommy has been working," Peaches lied cutting her eyes over to Chocolate. "It seems like your aunt is hiding secrets on when you're around love. That makes it kinda hard."

Placing a hand on her hip, Chocolate laughed. "Bitch you ain't been trying to get that baby. She been with her daddy and he's been doing both jobs as a parent. Maybe if you weren't running around with his friend you could have a moment to spend with, Kimmi."

"Bitch, I'll beat you." Peaches rushed over to her"

Jumping in between them, Kimmi's grandmother held up her hands. "I'll be damn if y'all pull this in front of my grandbaby. Somebody better gain some sense in this house before I slap the hell out one of y'all."

"I have the right to know when my daughter is around. I'm taking her with me," Peaches snapped waving her hand in the air.

"You ain't taking her nowhere. Tipton will handle all that with you. I brought her over here to see mama." Chocolate grabbed Kimmi's hand.

"What! You can't deny me, my baby. Fuck Tipton!" she screamed.

"Exactly, that ain't what the lawyer said. According to that drug test, you just failed. She belongs to Tipton unless you wanna go to court." Watching her grab Kimmi's hand to leave, she turned to face her. "You and Dejuan are wrong for what y'all doing. It's crazy because I introduced you to him and you still didn't achieve anything. Now you're mad because that boy is doing good for himself. Take some time and reflect on yourself," she said before leaving out the door.

"You just gonna sit there and watch her take my child?" Peaches looked at her mother with tears crumbling down her face.

"Peaches I'm sorry, but she's right. Look at yourself girl. That baby needs you and you running around like she ain't even in this world. Ever since I saw you running with that boy. It's been shit flying from everywhere. He's trouble and it's bound to dig you in a hole with him if you don't quit while you're ahead."

"You don't even know him. Y'all plotting against me and now my own mama is telling me that I don't need my child. You can roll over and kick rocks with their ass." Peaches headed for the door.

"You set your own path girl. You ain't doing nothing but shortening your days with all that disrespect. Look at yourself cause I damn sho didn't raise you that way." Her mom pointed a stern finger.

"Whatever, stop sitting back trying to act like you been a mother forever. I had to get it from somewhere," she shot back before slamming the door on her way out.

Chris Green

Chapter 11

"So, let me get this straight. You want me to go up to California? Make this girl give up her territory to let our workers run the spots, and force them to move more dope?" Chocolate asked with a raised eyebrow.

"Exactly," Tipton said pacing around the kitchen of her home.

All he could do was ponder on the recent phone call with Dejuan. It was clear that the gloves were off. He just hoped his mind didn't think to react with a stupid response because shit was gonna get worse. Looking at his daughter asleep on the soft leather couch, he remembered it was all for her. Including the family, there wasn't a day that he didn't wake up to achieve that goal. It was the only priority that mattered the most.

"Hell, you might as well rob and kill everybody then, Tipton. That's some deep shit and I don't think nobody is willing to just turn their hands over to you like that. What the hell are we gonna do if it goes totally wrong?" she replied.

"It won't, the three people who are on the list already has positions in that state. It's no one over or under them. Once we arrive there. The approach alone will force a decision out. It's either earn more money with us or die and lose it all. It's a mind trap. Sleepy doesn't really see the power he could push around. You have to make decisions. Shit that's gonna makes us sit back and give orders. Once the head falls—"

"The body crumbles," Halo finished his sentence.

"He's right, the game is simple. Once you strategize a plan to take control you got to enforce it. It's like the Navy. Once the seal tells us to seize. We're not stopping until shit is under control. It's the first strategy of war," Sonya clarified before taking a seat next to Halo.

"Uh, who the hell are you?" Chocolate asked with a funny expression.

"I'm me, you can just act like I'm an extra tattoo for this fine piece of specimen, right here." She rubbed a hand through Halo's wavy hair.

"Chocolate focus, crazy. This is serious," Tipton snapped his fingers. "I'm sending you because I know you'll be straight to the point. This isn't an option, Sonya will be right along your side to assist you with any troubles."

Chocolate rolled her eyes over to Sonya with a smirk. "What can she do that I can't?"

"She can pull a trigger. Now cut the foolery and pay attention. The men that I'm sending you with will remain behind once you know the rules are enforced. That will guarantee that all business is sufficient. We let our men go and regroup more workers. It'll eventually become our state. That's your mission, Halo, already has Nebraska. Demon will stay here to assist me."

"Now I been quiet and holding this blunt for the past two minutes. Where the hell does that leave me at in this equation?" Rex stepped back into the kitchen looking at him with a stern face.

Tipton rubbed his goatee. "You're gonna handle a special clientele. He's right here in, Georgia. The same goes for him also, enforcer the rules. If he bucks handle the business and place our blueprints on the big desk."

"Sounds good to me. Do we get to keep these niggas bitches and shit?" Rex smiled wickedly.

"Unless you wanna catch a rape charge. I'll advise you to just stick with the plan." Tipton dismissed his remark and took a seat.

"Smooth. Chocolate, I'm about to go take a shit in your pretty ass bathroom. I might need two rolls of tissue." Rex departed from the crew to head upstairs.

Tipton couldn't help but smile at Chocolate's screwed up face. His team was surely one to remember, with the right guidance and movements. The crew would be relaxing and pushing the necessary buttons without breaking a sweat.

"So, when does all this take place? Because I need to go shopping and hit a few beaches before I come back to this slave master ass state?" Chocolate questioned.

Taking a second to ponder on the question. He had to be sure that it was the right answer. "Tomorrow I want you all to close down any shops. Prepare the workers to leave. I used a couple of connections and got a few private jets for a decent price. We can move how we need to for about two weeks. So, we have to make this count. You'll leave the following day," Tipton said.

"Sounds great to me. I just wanted you to know that I did what you requested. That'll put a stump in his business because he depends on that section of the city," Sonya confirmed.

"Good, I'm sure you will be of good assistance with Chocolate also. There is no expense that you will ever have to worry about. Plus, your protection will be phenomenal. I just have one question?" Tipton asked curiously.

"What would that be?"

"Why are you doing this? I mean if you turned on Vel so fast. What makes it clear that you won't do the same to us?"

"Easy, satisfaction, I don't have to be loyal to anyone. I do it because I choose too. Right now, I'm on my own mission." She smiled before looking over to Halo.

Nodding with approval, Tipton smirked. "Welcome to the family then."

****

"I wanna know what the fuck happened to my shit and I mean now!" Vel yelled as he paced around his living room with two guns in hand.

The entire security team, down to the corner hustlers were standing at attention. No one made a sound.

"I asked a question that has yet to be answered. Can anybody tell me how in the fuck my best two movers was killed? Not to mention I wasn't robbed. My fucking money was burned. Four-hundred-fifty grand was set on fire. And you mean to tell me we don't know how it happened?"

Pulling the hammer to his gun back, he looked around at all the men. "So, who's ready to die first? Maybe we can solidify this quickly!"

"Boss, we have to narrow down this shit. It's only a few that know the stash spots and whereabouts of that crib. Everybody ain't did this shit," one of the men announced as he stood up straight off the wall.

Pointing his gun at the man's leg, Vel released one slug. *Boom*!

The force of the gun caused him to crumble down with ease before releasing a horrible scream. "Aaaggghhhh!"

The tension was now at its peak and all the men postures became stiff wondering who would be next. Vel was about to speak but caught his tongue once his cell began to ring. He stepped away from the large crowd, answered and placed the phone to his ear.

"Yeah!"

"I thought we were gonna handle that today? You still haven't made time," the man spoke through his line.

He exhaled and chuckled. "I'm a businessman, you know this. I'm caught up with a few things. That can always come."

"You said that before. It's crazy how money can make you

abandon your own responsibilities. That shit means nothing, bro. This is where your head has been ever since we've linked back in. What's the fucking problem now?"

"Do you hear yourself? I'm a drug dealer not a cashier for target. This is a twenty-four-hour job."

"Nigga you're a fucking dad. You need to try being one because you damn sho' ain't act as if I'm not living! I should've listened to my grandma when she told me that you were some bullshit."

"I don't have time for this. You're my son. Not a female, act like it," Vel replied before he hung up the phone.

Turning back around to face the hired employees. He cleared his thoughts before speaking, "Out of twenty years of doing this shit I've never had anybody take nothing from me. This was different, more personal. Has anybody seen this nigga, Dejuan?"

Everyone continued to remain quiet.

"I'm gonna make this clear as possible. I want bodies and I mean, right fucking now. Find this clown ass nigga and bring his ass to me. Find out what the fuck happened to my shit, and don't return with a closed mouth. That goes for everybody in this room."

Looking over at his next top shooter. Vel walked over to him. "Stretch this one on you, my nigga. You said you wanted your shot. Here it is, make that shit look good and don't come back until it's handled. When you do that, bring that ungrateful bitch ass nigga Tipton to me.

"Vel, you know I got you, blessings, Big Dog," the young killer ceased the conversation.

"All y'all niggas get the fuck out my crib. We got one week to take this shit down. By choice or by force. Stretch, I know how you move, and this is important. It's only two people who know about the details of that spot. My son is one of them. He's not even built for this life so I'm not even gonna let that cross my mind."

"Who else?" Stretch asked confused

"Sonya, I'll tell you this. If that hoe ain't no ghost when you see her. I want you to make that bitch wish she was dead. Cut her fucking head off," Vel said with a psychotic expression.

"That's my word, it's handled," Stretch mumbled before walking off.

Vel looked down at the young hustler who still clutched onto his leg in pain.

"I'm sorry, but you fucked up," he said before placing a bullet through his heart.

Boom!

****

It was seven in the morning when Tipton continued to hear his doorbell ring repeatedly. He jumped from his sleep, reached over Janita and grabbed his gun from the black nightstand.

"Baby who is that?" She shuffled in the bed.

"I don't know, just stay here," he whispered before heading out of their bedroom door.

After easing down the hallway, he spotted Halo. Looking out of the peephole of the front door. "Who is it?"

"Sincere, God. Did you tell him the address or something?"

"Hell nah, let him in." Tipton waved his hand while walking down the steps.

Halo opened the front door and stepped to the side so he could enter. "Damn, y'all niggas gonna let me wait out on the front porch forever? The temperature is dropping like a motherfucka!"

"How the hell did you find the house?" Tipton asked seriously.

"Duh nigga, Janita. How else was I supposed to find y'all if you ain't answering the damn phone?" Sincere said before taking a seat on the new Suede couch. "I see you found another crib. This shit nice."

"Yeah, it is. It's only temporary," Tipton mumbled before taking a seat next to him. "If you would've handled business and came straight back from Miami you could have been alerted on what we have in process."

"Bro, that shit ain't easy. Driving back and forth down to Florida like I deliver tuna for a fucking living. I be having to get a little chill time in. I mean it's the state for beaches and bitches. I wanna get my fun in, too," Sincere said as he removed his coat.

"It's not about that, Sincere. We move precisely. If you wanna go on vacation. Don't do it in the mix of business. That's all I'm saying. What will happen if you get caught up with something or if a nigga jack you for all that dough while ya moving sloppy down there? Secure the bag, then you play. It's just to make sure you're covering all your steps."

"I feel ya, bro." He nodded.

"Halo and Chocolate is about to leave for a few days on a business trip. That leaves me, you, and Rex to handle this while their away. After everything is in effect, shut down every shop for good. Those workers will now only be paid for one thing."

"What's that?"

"Killing, we need security. It's chess, not checkers. More soldiers mean more territory, more money, and more respect. I'm trying to capitalize, not lose. You can continue to work your move in Miami but soon you'll have to place the proposition to your connect."

"*Proposition*, what do you mean? We already do good business with each other," Sincere stated.

"And that's cool, but right now we on something different. The prices will drop but the territory will have to become ours. We will front them a certain amount of dope and use our hustlers to get it off in their state. Once we expand with our people. We will take it all," Tipton ran down the game plan quickly.

"Are you crazy? This man runs one of the biggest states in the South. Tipton, we don't even have the right amount of men to try something like that. This man has the police in his pocket. The community is being extorted from his businesses, and he's practically serving half of Miami. Kenny is not going for it."

"You sound confident about this dude. In the end, he's your clientele. I've never met this nigga and I could care less about who he's working with. This is a winning opportunity for him to win. All we want is a spot to push our product. We will drop the prices to ensure that they are receiving a nice portion off the top. It's no debating," Tipton informed.

"So, you just want me to muscle this man out his shit? You messing up my face. I'm the one driving back and forth down here to serve this nigga. Not you, bro."

"Cool, then you'll purchase bricks whole price from me for seventeen and serve him how you choose. I'm not trying to be hard, but it seems like you ain't good with listening bro. It's the way things gotta be to ensure that we all eat."

"*Seventeen*! Bro, what the hell has gotten into you?"

"I think I should be asking you the same thing?"

Shaking his head in disbelief, Sincere stood to leave. "Fine, I'll do what you said whenever I deliver his next shipment. I just want you to know that if anything goes wrong.

It's your fault, not mine."

"You have to remember that life isn't perfect. We're here to make an opportunity. Not wait for it to come and find us. If you think that it's too hard to handle. We can always just give up and do something different. It wouldn't matter to me," Tipton said before running a hand through his waves.

"Bet."

After watching him leave out of the door, Halo quickly locked it behind him. "You sure you want me to leave you here with these idiots, God?"

"I'm positive, bro. We need this. All you have to do is lay the foundation and come straight back."

"Whatever you say, God," he replied before heading back upstairs with Sonya.

Tipton gazed around the new four-bedroom home that he purchased with the help of Sleepy. It was far from the outskirts of Atlanta. One where only the true family would know about. The time for millions could be smelled a mile away and he wanted every piece that came toward him. All he wanted was to cater to Janita, Kimmi, and the team. Unfortunately, he didn't know that it was truly no love when it came to the dirty ones, he called family.

"Daddy, can I come and lay down with you?" Kimmi broke him out of his trance.

Standing with a stuffed animal in hand, she flashed him a bright smile.

"Of, course you can, Princess. Come here." He held out his arms.

She ran over to him, climbed on the couch and placed her head against his chest then embraced her into a warm hug. He cherished the feeling of how good it was to be a father. To have a purpose, Kimmi was the reason he strived to have everything his mom worked to give him, *the world.*

Chris Green

Chapter 12

Downtown Atlanta: 10:05 a.m.

"Just like I told y'all, dumb ass motherfuckers. I came home and found them like that?" Why in the fuck would I want to hurt my mother and sister?" Dejuan spat as he twisted his wrists from the irritating handcuffs.

"We're just making sure son. This is a delicate case. Your mother is in critical condition at the hospital and your sister is dead. The detectives are trying to look at this from every angle," The young officer responded.

Detective, Sandra, stepped in the room, holding a small brown profile folder. "I'll handle it from here officer, you're dismissed."

"Yes, ma'am."

Dejuan watched him leave out, then stared at the old woman in front of him. "I hope you're not here to ask no more questions because I'm tired of fucking taking."

"Nah, I'm not here to ask anything. I'm here to make you aware you, that's all"

"Of what? I've been in these cuffs for over sixteen hours and y'all still ain't released me. I'm already aware of everything I need to know."

"Well, actually, you're not. See we've been searching high and low for you dealing with this shooting that occurred about four months ago. I'm sure you Louie Gang members are really hard to stick out. Except for the tattoo that all of you have on the wrist. I mean, that's just a dead giveaway," Detective Elliot said before taking a seat.

Dejuan pulled his arms off the table and looked her square in the eyes. "I don't know what you're talking about."

"Oh, I'm quite sure you do. But I'm not here to speak on

111

Chris Green

that. It's actually the least of my worries. I'm looking for something different, like a drug dealer."

"I don't know any drug dealers," he lied.

Flipping over her folder, she slid a picture of Dejuan and Tipton across the table. "How do you know this guy, right here?"

Dejuan stared down at the photo, then tooted his nose. "I don't know that nigga. Musta been at a party or something."

"We got this off your Facebook page. The caption says that's my brother forever. Boss shit only. You're sure that's not a person you know?"

Remaining quiet, Dejuan shook his leg while staring at the ceiling.

"The reason I ask is because we're investigating the murder of his aunt. She was found with her head bashed in a while back, messy scene. The crazy shit about it is, we found your DNA inside her mouth. Is that something you wanna tell me about?"

"I've been fucking Lisa since I was a teenager. That shit was probably from a year ago. She's a fucking crackhead, lady. All them folks suck dick, duh!" Dejuan shouted with anger.

"And that's very understandable, I can't vouch for how many dicks a junkie can swallow for a hit. But I can vouch for how many murders I have seen dumb asses slip with like yourself."

"I didn't kill that bitch!"

"I didn't ask you that?" Detective Elliot responded. "I just wanna know about this guy." She pointed down at the photo of Tipton.

****

112

The sound of their bedroom door opening caused Janita to roll over. She gazed up at Tipton, then sat up. "Who was it?"

"Your brother," he replied before flopping down on the bed.

"Where's, Kimmi?"

"In her room, she fell asleep on the couch with me. I was placing other things in order, too. We need to think about where you wanna open a new shop. I was pondering on Cali."

"Tipton, all my family is down here. They're not gonna come all the way out to California for my exhibits." Janita brushed the hair from her face.

"I'm sure they will, I'll pay for it." He smiled.

Her beautiful brown eyes were so mesmerizing when she stared at him. Her cheeks would rise and show her deep kissy dimples. Janita was perfection in Tipton's mind. The loyalty was so pure. The love passed genuine, and she was all the above when it came to the perfect soulmate. Wisdom was something his mother exposed fluently while raising him. It was knowledge of protecting the black woman's heart. Impurity in a relationship would poison the heart of a woman within a small amount of time. Most would feel that impurity would be the minors, but it was more sacred. It was wise never to sleep with a man because of the way your feelings flutter for them. It was knowledge to never commit until you were sure he would also cherish you for eternity. There was only one soulmate for every person, and Janita was his.

"Why you always making me blush, boy? Get yo' cute ass on." Janita snickered.

Tipton slid the cover from her body, grabbed her legs and pulled her closer.

Dividing her smooth thick thighs, he lusted off her beautiful plump kitty." She panted. "I was about to go back to sleep, Tipton."

Chris Green

"I know, that's what we about to do," he mumbled seductively. He leaned down, slid his tongue quickly across her love button.

"Babyyy…sss…wait!"

"No." Tipton ignored her pleas and continued his mission.

Exploring every part of her, he folded her legs back for a better view, enjoying the sight of satisfaction. He moved his tongue and mouth from side to side. Janita's body shuddered, his warm lips caressed in between her sweet peach tightly.

She gasped, she could feel Tipton sliding his tongue inside. The way he slithered it at a fast pace forced her to moan, "Babyyy!"

Massaging her breasts gently, he could see her pupils roll in satisfaction. She was ready to cum, and he wasn't about to miss one fucking drop.

Sensing her energy, he wrapped his arms around her legs. His pace began to speed up his as she arched her back. Once her fingers clutched on to the bedsheets. He nibbled lightly on her pearl forcing the biggest orgasm she'd ever experience.

"Daddyyy!"

Of course, she began to jerk. So, Tipton placed a firm grip on her hips before slowly catching her sweet honey with his tongue.

"I need you here with me, Nita. You gotta stay right here beside me. No matter what," Tipton said while dropping his sweats to the floor.

"I promise," she moaned as he mounted her gently.

****

After a few hours of relaxation, Tipton left his home with Halo directly beside him. He was pondering on the task at hand, and before he sent everyone on their missions out of town. He wanted to check in with his business partner. The afternoon wind was hawking, and the Halloween decorations appeared more as they drove towards Sleepy's home.

"I've never seen so many weird ass people, God. You celebrate a holiday that you know nothing about. Murders, evil deeds and deception. They enjoy being tricked but will kill you about hearing the truth."

Trying to soak in Halo's theory, Tipton nodded lightly. He was always so damn deep when it came to the real world. "Everybody got to believe in something, Halo. Sometimes it's just about the world going around. We are only put here to do one thing. Live, but we're also obligated to dying, bro. Who's to say your happiness ain't sacred?"

"Whatever you say, God."

The ride was smooth, and the fellas coasted to Sleepy's house in a timely fashion. He parked the car directly in front of the pathway of his home. Tipton and Halo stepped out, as always, the butler was the first to appear before they could knock.

"Damn, you don't play." Tipton laughed holding out a hundred-dollar bill to him.

Grabbing the money with the tip of his fingers, he placed it lightly into his jacket pocket. "So, true, Sir."

Leading them inside, he announced them as usual before departing from the living area. Rika was wrapped into the seventy-inch plasma above her, and Sleepy sat on the gigantic wrap around sofa with a Stocks magazine in his hands.

"Tipton, I didn't know if it would be too late before you got my message. I'm glad you're here." He stood to greet him and Halo.

"Yeah, I tried to make due on this contract. We can't sleep forever," he replied.

Rika walked over to Tipton and placed a kiss on his lips.

"Are me and you still friends?"

Silence filled the room as Halo, and Sleepy turned their heads.

"Uh, yeah Rika, of course, we're friends. Why would that change?" Tipton stumbled over his words.

"Because I heard that you a real married man now. Can you come check on me before you leave? I'm in the room to the far back," she answered with puppy-like eyes.

"Uh, sure."

"Thanks love." She smiled before departing from the guys.

"Okay, like I was saying." Sleepy smirked with a nod. "I know business is now in effect. You said there was a plan you got in mind. Was it necessary for me to hear it, or was it a silent movement?"

"Nah, it's nothing silent about it. I'm in it for capitalism. I want to enforce the same on the ones who work with us. Someone has to take the lead." Tipton held firm eye contact.

"Understood, but where does Capitalism fit into our clientele? They already purchase from us. That means we should be looking for more customers using their help."

"Exactly, but instead of asking, I'm going to make them. It's a difference."

Catching onto his statement, Sleepy smiled. "I understand how things could switch in the mix of business. As long as you're comfortable enough to handle what comes behind it."

"That's the only way I know." Tipton shrugged.

"Well, I guess I didn't need to have a meeting with you. When are you planning on making your move?"

"Today." He grinned before shaking Sleepy's hand.

Chapter 13

Eighteen Hours Later: Omaha Nebraska

Halo pulled his large Suburban down his designated street and pressed his breaks forcing the four trucks behind him to halt. He looked around the cold area, his eyes landed on the four men posted outside of Milo's spot. Omaha was a different kind of city. It was a state where everyone loved to shoot for fun, no matter who it was. The reality wouldn't kick in until they stood over a person to find out you might have killed a close relative or even a friend. It was that type of state.

So, there was no time to waste when it came down to enforcing his hand. Halo stepped out into the cold weather, adjusted his skull cap and whistled. The four black trucks behind him began to rock back and forth as the big group of men exited the vehicles. They were heavily armed with assault rifles, and none of these motherfuckers looked like they went a day without catching a damn murder.

As he walked up to the thirty-man crew, Halo nodded. "Fifteen of y'all come with me. The other half, surround the spot." As they moved in compliance, Halo proceeded toward the front door of Milo's spot.

The men in his yard shuffled nervously as the massive crew barged through their front yard and walked past his workers as if they were invisible. Halo knocked sternly on the door.

It didn't take long before Milo answered with a shocked expression. "Yo' what the fuck are all yall niggas doing on my doorstep. You couldn't just bring one man? Cause all them ain't coming in here."

"I'm coming in alone, God. They all can wait out here." Milo clutched on his gun before stepping to the side. After

Chris Green

Hall entered the house. He closed the door and applied the latches. "What happened to ya boy? Thought he was supposed to be coming?

"Nah, change of plans, God, I'm handling the business."

"Cool, my boss man is right in the living area. Aye Shine, we got the businessman here for ya."

Shine came into the large room, raised his vision and locked eyes with him. "Halo?"

"Wassup, Shine, long time no see God."

He walked over and embraced Halo in a brotherly hug. "Look at my little brother. You all grown up and shit now. You know I wasn't entitled to send you shit when you fucked up like that. It hurt me to see you sit in that prison in Georgia, but you look good. What you doing here?" Shine questioned.

"Hold up, y'all know each other?" Milo was looking confused.

"Yeah, he's my foster brother. We was raised in the same house until he decided to kill my dad and sent all relations down shit creek. But hey, things are moving sweet for me in Nebraska. How in the hell did you find me?"

"He's here for the plug. The nigga from Georgia," Milo butted in.

"What, you're the plug?"

"Call me whatever you want, God. Are we doing business or not?"

"Well, I be damned, I see you moving on up. Who would of thought, I'd be negotiating prices with my little brother? Please take a seat, let's talk business," Shine said before heading back to his spot.

"I'll stand. It's quite simple what the rules are gonna be so it shouldn't be long." Shine looked over at Milo with a curious expression.

Shine placed a cigarette between his lips and sparked the

lighter. "Rules, I've never been too good with those. Are you sure you're trying to sell dope?"

"I'm positive, God. The money we deduct from your prices will benefit you generously. We want the territory you control in Omaha only to move more product. We have our own men, and we will continue to hire more until we can pick up the whole state."

Shine chuckled and clapped his hands. "Hold up, hold up! You telling me, you want me to buy dope from your plug? Place his workers in my spots, and give him a cut?

"Exactly."

"Tell that nigga to suck my dick!" Shine spat. "I'm not a lame. I push my weight through sixty percent of this city. I ain't never needed help, and my circle is tighter than insect pussy. You either gonna sell me the keys for a better price or rise the fuck up out of my spot. That sounds like a bad mistake to even speak on some shit like that in my presence."

"There is no debating. That's what God offered you, and its proceeding with, or without you," Halo confirmed, standing from his seat.

Shine folded his arms. "So, what the fuck you trying to say lil' bro? You saying, you taking my shit?"

Halo pulled out his Springfield 45 handgun and put a bullet through the center of his forehead. His lifeless body gasped for air. The movement of his lips showed him sliding into the afterlife before dropping to the floor. Milo quickly jumped in the corner with his head against the floorboard. The knots in his stomach was turning so bad that he passed gas as Halo rolled him over.

"Please don't fucking kill me, man. I don't know what the fuck he did but it wasn't me!" he screamed out of fear.

"I won't, I just need you to listen. All this shit in here belongs to the boss. You have a chance to eat and remain alive.

Make the money, pay it on time, and watch it grow. My crew will stay here to assist you. They will hire more men as we go to ensure that you're not getting the wrong ideas. Say it, this spot belongs to the boss." Halo placed the gun to his skull.

"This spot—belongs to the boss!" Milo fumbled before spitting it out.

"Good, I'll have a shipment delivered tomorrow. Remember if things go wrong, it falls on you."

"I understand, nigga, you just clearly showed me that."

Halo turned on his heels to leave, his eyes wide with seriousness before he exited the home. As Halo stepped outside, his men were aiming their weapons at Shine's rookie bodyguards.

He moved through the crowd, stopped and looked at them all. "Y'all make amends and squash your beef you're coworkers now. It was nice doing business with you guys." He smirked before climbing back in his Suburban. Then he smashed off through the street, headed back to the airport so he could catch his flight.

The instrument of death was a tool that conquered mostly all, the mighty gun. Although, it implied the fear that was needed. There weren't too many niggas who could use it the correct way. Certain people were meant to die from the roots of their own evil. It was the only way to balance sins. Halo was the angel of death that would ensure it flowed no different.

He dialed Tipton's number on his cell, pressed call and placed the phone to his ear?

"Waddup, bro?"

"It's handled, God. You can put everything in place."

"That was quick. Catch you a hotel and fly back in the a.m. I want you to stick around for the night just in case. If all is still even, I'll see you by morning."

"Whatever you say, God," Halo agreed before ending the call.

****

Los Angeles California

Hearing the sharp knock on her door, Kima quickly closed her legs and covered up the small masturbation toy. "What the fuck is it?"

She watched her trusted bodyguard step inside, he moved over to her bed. "The meeting you put in place, they're here."

"What, I thought that was tomorrow?"

"No, they're waiting down in your office, right now. I didn't want to bother you because I knew it was your day off, but it's business."

"Damn it!"

She slanged the small rubber penis across the room and jumped out of the bed to retrieve some clothes. "I can't ever bust a nut around this bitch without being needed for something. Tell them I'll be down in a second. You can remove yourself."

Shaking his head slowly, the guard exited the room and closed the door behind him.

After twenty minutes of freshening up, Kima made her way downstairs to the bottom floor office. As she walked inside, she paused upon seeing Chocolate and Sonya. "Uh, who the hell are y'all?"

"Uh, we're here for the meeting on behalf of, Tipton," Chocolate replied sarcastically.

"Tipton, I'm not set to meet with him until next week." Kima folded her arms.

"Well, I'm afraid we were told different, baby girl. I

already had a hard time getting through your fake ass security. So, we need to sit down and come to an agreement on a few things."

Sitting down on the edge of her desk, she cleared her throat. "I don't know if you heard me or not, Sweetie, but I don't have time to be playing with a few worker hoes. I have money to make. Like I said, I'll meet with that little boy next week. Get up and get the fuck out of my house," Kima spat with venom.

Standing to her feet, Chocolate invaded her space until they stood face to face. "Look, you pimp squeak ass bitch. That man sent me up here to do one thing. Tell you that we're dropping these prices and we're moving workers inside your shit. You can lay back and watch your money be made while we control this movement, or you can shut down shop. Make a choice before I beat yo' ass!"

Sonya stepped between them, placing a hand on Chocolate's chest. "Can you let me speak to her alone, please? That's not the way you handle business."

"What? That bitch yelling at us like she crazy. We got money to hoe."

"You have to excuse her. This has been a long ride and we really would like to come down to this agreement." Sonya flashed Kima a phony smile.

"Doesn't sound like y'all wanna speak business, how she's talking. I'm not moving any workers in the mix of my shit. I don't know who y'all take me for, but I'll have y'all bitches head on a platter within seconds." Kima smirked with arrogance.

"By who, bitch?" Chocolate shouted. "I hope you ain't referring to them ten bitch ass bodyguards who stretched out in your front parking lot? Your house has been surrounded for the past thirty minutes, dumb ass girl."

Kima laughed, stepped towards the blinds and peeped out. The sight of her team sitting on their knees at gunpoint forced a lump in her throat. The masked men that surrounded her home glared directly at the window causing her to close them quickly.

"Why is he doing this? I explained at the meeting that I didn't need any help doing anything. You're not the only ones with a trick up your sleeve."

Sonya cut her eyes to Chocolate. "Give me five minutes and I'll be out. Chocolate snatched up her purse and huffed. "Bitch you got five minutes or I'ma sweep this whole damn house up the street."

Stepping out of the office, Chocolate closed the door and stood in the center hallway. Not only was she irritated, but the fact of being in California, and not having any fun was starting to put a wedgie in her ass. It was unheard of to make money and spend it on nothing. The point of stepping into the game was to live the life. Not to hide and cuff the money like a bitch is great granny.

The sounds of light moans flowed through her eardrum breaking the lavish thoughts. Wiggling a finger around her earlobe. She listened harder and heard the same.

"Ssss, right there."

Easing back toward the office, Chocolate placed her head against the door. Surely, she could hear the chum bucket bitch Kima panting for dear life. Sonya had some fucking nerve to get her a private pussy date in the mix of business while shit was about spiral out of control. Before Chocolate could pull out her phone to call Tipton. Sonya was walking out of the office with a small line of sweat running from her forehead.

"We can go now, everything is good," Sonya assured with a wide grin.

"What the hell were you doing?"

Chris Green

Before Sonya could reply, Kima came and posted in the doorway. Her hair was messy and her chest heaved up and down before she spoke, "Tell that dog ass nigga, Tipton, he ain't getting nothing but twenty percent, and I hope his ass got somewhere for all them niggas to sleep cause they ass ain't crashing here," she spat before slamming her office door.

Sonya grabbed Chocolate's arm and pulled her towards the front door. "We can go now, our job is done."

"Bitch, I wanna know what you was doing in that room. I heard that hoe moaning. What happened?"

"It's simple, she's gay, I'm a lesbian. I can tell by the way she was acting behind closed doors. She a freak of nature in the open, it's all business," Sonya replied as they walked out of the home.

As they passed their armed men, Chocolate nodded giving them the okay to stand down. "I'll say this before I leave. We are a team, and it's gonna be great doing business with you guys. My name is Chocolate and I'm your new boss," she announced before climbing in the vehicle with Sonya to leave.

Chapter 14

Decatur Georgia: 5:30 p.m.

Biggs inhaled on his blunt slowly as he looked over the large balcony, sipping on his cup of clear Vodka. He turned to see his wife heading for him. Knowing it was about to be an argument, he downed the last of his liquor.

"Biggs, I know you saw me calling your phone fat ass motherfucker!"

"Watch yo mouth, bitch. I ain't even in the mood, Tiara."

"Nah, fuck you! I'm minding my business, spending money and shit in the mall. Guess who slid they happy ass up on me? Ya stanky ass, baby mama. According to her, you were all up in that pussy night before last. The same night you had to go check on yo' boy's mama, right?"

"Man, you really sat here and let Pooh tell you some shit like that, and you believed it? You deserve to be a dumb wife," he spat before inhaling the weed again.

"Fuck you, bitch. Ya ugly turtle looking ass, baby mama the one who needs you, not me." Tiara turned on her heels to leave.

"Bye, bitch," Biggs mumbled before leaning back against the rail.

Just when his mind began to zone out. He spotted five black Tahoe trucks pulling into his driveway.

"What the fuck!" he said under his breath before gripping the handle of his gun.

As the first truck stopped, Biggs watched as Rex stepped out and looked up into his eyes. "Say, Fatman, is it cool if we talk about some business? I'm making a quick stop for, Tipton."

"Me and Tipton don't got no business. I explained that to

Sleepy already!" Biggs spat. He pulled his weapon so it could be shown that no bitch was in his blood.

After sixteen men dispersed from the vehicles in his driveway. Rex shook his head. "I think we do, bro. I promise it won't take long and it'll be worth your time."

Sensing that shit was real, he gritted his teeth and headed downstairs.

"Bae, who the fuck are those men in my driveway?" Tiara looked out of the window in fear.

"Just stay in the house. Call, Beezy, and let him know to get his ass over here with the crew now!" he whispered before walking out the front door.

Moving towards Rex and his men, he stopped about six feet away with a stern mug. "You niggas ain't got no business being here. I'm not doing nothing with that young fool, and I made that clear."

"First of all, calm down. No one has come at you in a belligerent manner, Papa Smurf. I'm only delivering a message, Sir."

All Biggs could do was eye the armed men who stood behind Rex. Their demeanors didn't seem too friendly, and not too many people wanted to have a friendly convo when guns were involved. "It seems like a nasty message the way you pulled up at my spot? I've never caused no problems y'all way. So, what's the catch?"

After lighting up a blunt, Rex started to cough violently from the strong marijuana. "Hell nah, you ain't do nothing, bro. It's just a little change in movement. So, we putting everybody on point who shop with us. From this day on, we dropping yo' prices down to nine a key."

"*Nine*? This can't be the same shit Sleepy was serving me. I pay thirteen."

"True, but Tipton is going to give them to you for nine. Of

126

course, there are some things that need to be agreed on, and that's why I'm here," Rex said before passing the joint to a man behind him.

"Like what?" Biggs mugged.

"For starters, your hood. We want it, we're gonna drop our workers in your spots because they are familiar with the recipe to flip it back. We will drop more product on them and hire more men to work. You get your cut right off the top and don't have to lift a finger. That's an easy check," Rex explained.

Biggs chuckled and took a step forward. The automatic rifles that raised towards his face paused his thoughts for a slight second.

"Hold up fellas, give Biggs a chance to set things even." Rex waved his hands for them to lower their guns.

"Nigga I been in this shit for over ten years. I ain't never held my hand out for not one nigga to feed me. I'm a negotiator, but I ain't never settled for anybody extorting me. Tipton isn't my dealer, Sleepy is."

"Not anymore, Tipton is running all this shit according to the big man. We don't make the rules, brother, we just follow them. We're not asking for your money. We only want our men in your territory to monitor some extra paper for us. Now if you're not hearing that. Then we wanna take it all," Rex said with a nonchalant shrug.

Taking a deep breath, Biggs thought about raising his pistol to blow Rex's brains across the pavement. Unfortunately, the angry heavily equipped shooters behind him made it quite difficult.

"Listen, man, we don't even need those types of problems floating around town. He's a businessman, just like my-self. I'm down for purchasing at the new prices but allowing him to invade on my movement is not about to happen. I'll die before I do that!"

"You sure about that?" Rex cocked a bullet into his chamber and placed it up to Biggs's nose.

Feeling the cold steel against his flesh caused him to fidget. The look in Rex's eyes stated that this would be the last moment he got to speak his peace. Humbling himself, Biggs realized he was in a position that he couldn't win at the time. Before he placed everything at risk. He took the smart route and agreed.

"I'll have something for him next week, but I'm not letting nobody take my hood, bro. That's the best I can do. If he can't work with the payments, then you might as well just go ahead and blow my brains out."

Smiling, Rex lowered his gun. "You ain't gotta even worry about all that, Mr. Teddy Gram. If he says different, I'll be pulling back down on yo' block to meet you in this same spot. But instead of sixteen, I'm gonna bring forty men with me to ensure that you ain't built up them little kibbles and bits in ya pants. I'm sure you will let this flow with ease. We don't need no foul play, correct?"

"Nah, nothing foul. I hear you," Biggs assured with his hands down by his side.

"Smooth," Rex smirked before stepping back into his truck.

The small army of men did the same and vacated back inside their trucks. Within a few seconds, Biggs was standing in his front lawn shaking like a dog's first time in the pound. Making his way back into the house.

Tiara held the phone up before whispering, "It's Beezy."

Grabbing the phone from her hand, He placed it to his ear. "Hello?"

"What's the problem?"

"Nothing, bro, just a slight misunderstanding," Biggs lied.

"*Misunderstanding*? Yo' girl said that niggas just put a

128

gun to ya head. You sure shit is okay?" Beezy questioned with authority.

Taking a second to respond, Biggs' eyed Tiara with hatred. "I'm sure, but I might need your help with something."

"I'll be through there tomorrow," he spoke through the line before hanging up the call.

Chris Green

Chapter 15

10:15 p.m.

As Vel pulled his Lexus truck inside of his six-bedroom home, he parked and sparked his cigar before stepping out. As he moved past a few of his trusted soldiers, they greeted him

"Wassup, Big Dog?"

Giving them a light nod, he continued to head inside of his crib and maneuvered past his doormen. One of them whispered into his ear, "You have a guest in the living area, Sir."

He hung his coat on the rack and puffed his Cubano. "*Guest*?" Instead of asking questions, he strolled smoothly to the designation.

As he walked into the family room, he spotted a few of his workers posted with their weapons as Tipton sat on the couch next to Demon. Feeling his heartbeat increase.

Vel smiled. "Well, I be damn, Mr. White is that you? After all this motherfucking run around beefing, you got the nerve to come in my spot. Tell me why I shouldn't shoot your ass, right now?" Vel puffed on his cigar.

"Because you need me." Tipton stood to his feet. "Regardless of past dealings, I've come to make my proposition, and after that, I'm letting it play out however you wish bro."

"*Proposition*? The only deal you can be making with me is whipping my keys for all this pain and suffering I've been put through. I've lost money, and some of my best people because of you. Let me give you this proposition, you either gonna work for me for free or I'ma kill you right here where you stand, along with ya little junkie friend, right here." He waved a hand towards Demon.

"And what if I don't wanna work for you?" Tipton asked with a straight face.

"Then I'll give you a better offer. Give me your recipe. Hand over all your assets and money. I'll allow you to leave the state and live if you'll agree to stay away forever." Vel leaned against his wall.

"I'm okay with working, because I'm not about to leave my state, but I'll only agree under one condition." Tipton held up a single finger.

Smirking, Vel shook his head. "One condition, huh? And what the fuck might that be?"

"I wanna know what that tattoo on your wrist means?"

Covering up the cursive L with his fingers, Vel looked Tipton up and down. "If I lose, you lose. You either in or you out?"

All the hittas stood around the room quietly as if they were waiting on Vel to snap a finger.

"I'ma tell you what's about to happen. I'm about to leave out that front door. Go home to my wife and child. I'm going to make love to my wife tonight while I'm thinking of the money I'm making. While I'm living it up with my entire team. You're not gonna even remember that you're dead. It's gonna be like a photo in your memory. You're gonna be dead still thinking of me old man. So, let me ask you a question. How do you wanna die?" Tipton asked calmly.

Laughing loudly, Vel turned in a full circle to make sure he wasn't hearing the insults and threats that were coming out of Tipton's mouth. "One of y'all please kill this young pussy, nigga!" he shouted.

The crowd in the living room stood still as if the order was never given. All his men held on to their weapons with a look of sympathy in their eyes.

"Y'all niggas can't hear! I said smoke this muthafucka!"

The loud laughter that erupted caused him to look around in confusion. Not only was it a serious heated moment, but his own killers were laughing harder than Tipton. The gut feeling told Vel what was coming next before he opened his mouth.

"See I have to explain this the best way possible. When I said you were going to die, I meant that. These guys standing around you. They think like me, I mean, why work for a nigga who chump me off with crumbs when I can make great money with the man who really stands on loyalty. See I made sure all their pockets were good with a real check. I ensured trust in them by making sure their families would be good forever. I showed real love. These guys work for me now."

"Fuck you!" Vel spit on Tipton's shirt.

The hard, right punch from a bald-headed gunman sent him crashing to the floor. Before he could jump up, there were six niggas on his ass, pistol-whipping and stomping him.

"I fed y'all. Nigga, I fed y'alll!" he screamed as the men showed no compassion with the beating.

Yawning lightly as he watched Vel get his ass kicked. Tipton snapped ceasing the small brawl. "Pick 'em up."

Two men slowly rose Vel up by the arms. Trying to stand on his limp noodle legs. He coughed up blood and his eye was swelling by the second. "I'm an O.G. lil' nigga. You'll never live no shit like this down fool. You ain't gonna be able to go nowhere," he spat through his broken teeth.

"I believe I will, Vel. See you thought you were slick. Like you could hide out in the fields and never be spotted. Trying your best to blend in with the rest. You're just like the other snakes, and distrustful motherfuckers who crawl on this earth. You killed my mama, pussy. You shot my mom in front of me when I was thirteen years old." Tipton was nearly in tears.

"Nigga, I'm your father. Why the fuck would I kill yo' mother? You can't give me one reason!" Vel was breathing harshly.

"Easy, jealously, Demon you can take care of your business. Make it slow and I'll meet you back at home," Tipton said before heading for the door.

Vel watched the scrawny, white man rise from the couch and began to put up a small struggle. "Indeed, sir." He tilted his head before removing a sharp razor blade.

As Tipton made his way outside. All he could do was smile after hearing Vel scream at the top of his lungs. The feeling was so grand. It was the ultimate payback. Especially for the torture, his mother went through when he was a child. The day her life was taken by a crooked ass nigga who was jealous about not getting any money. The tables always eventually turned, and the gun was now in the rabbit's hand.

He climbed inside his McLaren, sparked a blunt of marijuana and pulled out of the gated home.

****

After making it home, Tipton removed his coat and smiled at the sight of his sleeping wife on the couch. Her hands were wrapped around the remote as if she was watching her favorite episode of Killing Eve, and her pouting lips released a light snore every time she breathed. He sat down beside her and placed a line of kisses on Janita's cheek, down to her lips.

She opened her eyes, yawning before wrapping him into a tight hug. "Hey, Daddy."

Enjoying the smell of her soft curly hair. He exhaled, it felt so good to come home to a warm spirit. Most men spent their nights chasing women by the dozen. A few even still manage to go home miserable after having all the fun in the world. It was better to enjoy love. To find someone that you can really connect with. It was nothing like coming home to a wife. A strong black woman that would hold you down beyond the dirty streets. Tipton could actually sit back and say that he was one of luckiest men ever to fall for a woman like Janita.

"Hey, beautiful, I see that you was entertaining the couch while I was gone." He grinned before placing a kiss on her lips.

She giggled as she sat up. "Yeah, I was watching my show and next thing I knew it was watching my ass. How was your day?"

Thinking back to the screams of Vel ringing through his ears, Tipton nodded. "It was okay, nothing compared to how good it would've been if I spent it with you."

"Aww, you always know how to make me smile." Janita blushed.

Hearing the sharp knock on his door caused Tipton to stand up and remove his pistol. He placed a hand to his fingers for Janita to remain calm, crept over to the front door and glanced out of the peephole.

He released his hand from the trigger and placed the gun back on his waist. "It's your brother."

He opened the door and Sincere stepped in with a clueless expression. "I didn't interrupt y'all from doing no nasty shit did I?"

"Boy shut up." Janita stood to her feet and embraced her family. "I was just about to take a bath. So, I'll leave y'all to talk," she mentioned before heading up the stairs.

"Let me find out you don't wanna be around me anymore since you married, my boy." He laughed playfully.

"Shut up, Sincere!" She shouted before disappearing to the top floor.

"Waddup? I thought you was on your way to Miami?" Tipton asked before taking a seat.

"Yeah, I was, but Kenny called me today for another forty. I decided to go ahead and pick that up before I have to make a double trip."

"That's cool. Did you think about what I said?"

"Yeah, I did. It's a lot I been thinking about, and that's the reason why I came to talk with you. I'm not sure how he takes this tomorrow, but I'm going to do exactly what you said. Now if he agrees, I would like to purchase my own weight from you at whole price and do my own thing in Florida. I just feel like it'll be more opportunity down there for me, ya know? I'm starting to learn the area, meet new people. I just wanna build something of my own," Sincere said with a straight face.

Tilting his head with a slight shrug. Tipton's face showed no emotion. "If that's what makes you happy my guy. Shoot for it. All I'm worried about is my business. It wouldn't matter whether you or Kenny is buying them."

Raising his head, Sincere folded his arms. "So, you not mad at me?"

Forcing a light laugh, Tipton shook his head. "Why would I be mad at you? You're my boy, all I can say is we have to live with our decisions. Make the best one for yourself brudda. All I can do is try my best to stand behind you."

"That's real. After tomorrow I feel this shit is gonna be a new start for me. You know I had to come check in with you, but I'm about to get on the road to make this trip my boy." Sincere showed Tipton some love with a brotherly hug.

"Handle that, just be careful," Tipton stated before opening his front door.

"Always," he replied before stepping out into the thick night wind.

Chapter 16

Miami Florida: Kenny's Penthouse Suite

After making the long ass drive, Sincere jumped out of his car and finished the last of his red bull energy drink. He screwed up his face from the hot liquid, then tossed it to the side.

The parking lot of the hotel wasn't packed as usual. The sun was starting to protrude, and he didn't want to waste any time getting back to the city. He pulled the duffle bag from the trunk and looked around cautiously before closing it. The area was so quiet and calm it didn't take much to alert a motherfucka that you were doing some illegal shit. It was the reason Sincere played things cool upon every visit. Not only did he purchase his own room, but he networked with a few people to make his face familiar around the building. Now it was nothing out of the way happening when the administration of the property was aware of his connections with Kenny. The old grease ball was a golden ticket to do whatever the fuck he pleased.

After strolling through the large vestibule of the hotel. Sincere made his way to the elevators and headed for the top floor. The excitement of new money was all that ran through his mind while on the mission. He just didn't know how Kenny was going to take Tipton's new proposal.

As the elevator doors opened, he moved up to the bodyguard who held the position in front of the room. "Sincere, what's good my man. Kenny's waiting for ya."

"Thanks. He ain't got no strippers in this bitch do he?"

"You know, Kenny." the bulky man laughed with a shrug.

As he opened the door, Sincere's heart froze into a bulk of ice from the sight of eight drug agents aligned the room with their badges visible. Kenny rested in center of them fully clothed with a bulletproof vest. As he stood to his feet, Kenny shook his head. "Wassup, Sincere? I think we need to talk."

The sight of a badge connected to Kenny's hip made Sincere feel as if he was in a dream. The money, the women, it was all fake. Sincere glanced to the side of him. He spotted Cream holding her gun in hand. The entire room was filled with cops, and he happened to be the only oddball standing with forty keys of cocaine in his hands.

Thinking about making a run for it. He looked back into the eyes of the bodyguard who stood outside of the room. "Just close the door, Sincere. Don't make it harder on yourself. You won't make it," the man said before flashing him another shiny badge.

"Fuck!" he shouted sitting the bags on the floor.

Stepping face to face with him, Kenny smirked. "I'm sure you know by now that we aren't friends? I'm also positive that you know about the two hundred and fifty keys you've sold me over the time of our business. Now I'm not here to pick out any faults, but I need your help."

"Nigga you a fucking, fed! I trusted you. We had an agreement!" Sincere balled up his fists in anger. "What happened to the so-called team? The way we suppose to ate good in Miami until we couldn't eat anymore."

"Sincere, I'm a fucking cop. It was a lie, the golds, the image. It was all fake. I've never met a man that has produced more cocaine than you in all my years of working for the government. You screwed up, but there is a way to change all this. You have forty keys of cocaine sitting on my hotel floor, right now. I have recordings, videos of transactions, and money transfers dealing strictly with you. I know it may seem like the world has come to an end. Like the rest of your life will be spent inside of a cold cell, but it doesn't have to be that way."

Sincere stared around at the other officers and whispered only for Kenny to hear him, "I can't go to jail man. I have money, you can have all that shit. You can't do this shit to me, Kenny. Not like this," Sincere begged.

"First of all, my name is Agent Witherspoon, and I don't want to see you go down like this either, Sincere. I actually think you are a good kid, but you're in a tight spot. As I said, we need your help." He held up his arms trying to negotiate.

His jaws began to clench together. "What the fuck do you need my help with? This ain't my fucking dope, you know that Kenny."

"I know that I want the man who's in charge, Tipton," He said with a serious expression.

"I can't do that, they'll kill me!"

"I'm sorry, but I don't think you have too much of a choice left, Sincere. That's the best I can offer you. Now I know it probably feels uncomfortable talking to me. So, I'll let you sit down and discuss what you need with one of my coworkers. Things that will be kept confidential between you and her. All I need is your compliance. If not, I'm gonna have to proceed with the next option," Agent Witherspoon explained before pulling out his handcuffs.

Feeling a sense of fear erupt through his body. He wanted to break down and cry like a child. Still in all, it wouldn't relieve him from the drastic situation. He was tied down to a case that would surely bring a hundred years on the first plea. The thought of Tipton flashed vividly through his mind. They had been friends since middle school. It was a bond that could never be broken. From the fights, down to the money. Tipton remained by his side. Those times were officially at its end. "Who the fuck do I gotta talk to man?"

The older, white woman stood to her feet and proceeded over to him. "Hi, Sincere, My name is Detective Elliot. If you don't mind I'd like to speak with him alone," she requested while looking at the other agents.

"He's all yours," Agent Witherspoon replied before clearing the room. "We will be outside if you need us."

After watching the door close behind them, Detective Elliot switched her expression to a dark frown. "Listen, son, I'll be very clear just this one time. If I don't hear what I need. You'll be leaving here in the next ten minutes on the way to a federal holding facility. But if you can give me the facts, I need, I'll make sure you're in your car heading back for Atlanta within the next hour. Your choice."

"What all do you need?" Sincere said lowering his head.

"You can start off by telling me who's all involved with this operation."

Chapter 17

3:45 p.m.

The day was flowing smoother than ever. Janita was in the backyard hooking up the grill, ribs, burgers, and hotdogs were on the menu. Including the sides she prepared earlier throughout the day, Tipton assured her that the small celebration would be a moment of joy for them all. Not just for being great hustlers but staying down as a team. Everyone was back from handling their business. Halo, Sonya, and Chocolate. Even Rex was running around with a smile, something he hadn't seen from his best friend in a while.

Tipton stood up from his chair to make an announcement, "Say y'all, if it's not too much to ask. I need y'all to gather around this table and let me have a little word with y'all. It won't take long."

He watched all them abandon their activities. They took a seat around the large glass table. Janita came and took her place behind his chair. The outside deck was so beautiful that it caused Tipton to look around before speaking. "I would like to thank y'all from the bottom of my heart."

"For what, Chris Brown?" Rex chuckled while sparking a rolled doobie.

Tipton chuckled and shot him a bird. "Because fool, y'all mean the world to me. Without this operation, and family. I wouldn't have none of this."

"Awww, you finally see how hard I work my ass off for you, nigga?" Chocolate smirked through slanted eyes.

"I've always known, Chocolate. And I want to thank you more than anyone. Without your help, this shit would be on the ground. I damn near think you can take my spot."

"Boy, shut up. You know that's a lie." She blushed from

the compliment.

"Seriously, you're a big key to our success. That's the reason I got a gift for all of you. I placed three-hundred gees into a personal, and private accounts for everyone. It's money of appreciation. Nothing compares to where we will be in a few months."

"Ohhh, bitch, I'm buying me a Range Rover in the morning. That's my dream car." Chocolate rocked her legs excitedly.

"It's for you to splurge girl, but I'm sure you will handle that with no problem. Halo that goes for you to, bro. I need you to step out and have some fun with this cash."

"I'm just relaxing, God," he replied with a smile.

"He don't need nothing but this fun in between my legs. Money can come later." Sonya smiled scooting closer to him.

"I'm sure he will." Tipton chuckled. "All in all, y'all, we're winning, and there ain't no looking back. I dreamed of living my life this way one day. A day that I can say we will be good forever. Cherish these moments and understand that we might not be perfect, but we're good enough to make it happen when it comes to getting the job done."

"Yeah, so much for all us having that happy relationship you got. I feel like I'ma die as a fucking lesbo who loves cats and dildos." Chocolate frowned.

As everyone shared a laugh. Tipton stood up and followed Janita back to the grill. He wrapped his arms behind her. He placed a delicate peck on her neck. "Mrs. White, why do I get the feeling you're not having fun?"

"No, baby, I am," she lied to prevent the conversation that was coming.

Turning her around, he took the spatula from her hand and placed it on the grill. "No, talk to me. You're my wife. It's kinda clear when something is wrong with you. Share it with me?" Tipton asked sincerely.

She stared in his eyes and admired the handsome man that she grew to love. It was never in her vision upon meeting him that they would be married within eight months. Her entire world was flipped, and it was truly for the better. The only thing that worried her brain was his profession. The game, it was never guaranteed that he would walk through that door every night. It was a woman's biggest fear to watch their love be taken away for the sake of supplying the streets with poison.

"What will I do if I ever lose you?"

Moving the hair from her face. He gazed at her with a bright smile. "Lose me how, bae?"

"To the streets, Tipton. What if I wake up and get a call that you're not coming home to me and Kimmi. How am I supposed to get past that?"

"Baby, I'm not leaving you period. We're gonna grow old together, and we're gonna leave this world together. I don't give a damn what it may look like. I move this way for a reason. I'm gonna make it to where we can be across seas living while someone else is putting in all this dirty work. You don't hustle to keep doing the same thing Janita. You do it so when the right time presents itself, you can just quit. I refuse to see any of that happen because of me sticking around when I clearly see that we've made enough. Right now, we haven't made enough baby," he replied while grabbing ahold of her hand. "Stick with me, trust me, and watch how it plays out for us. Now let's go have some fun with everybody, so I can get my freaky time in peace with you tonight."

A wide smile spread across her face from his remark. She kissed his lips, they both headed back for the table to enjoy the rest of their night.

The time was remarkable when it came down to his family

and team. It was a sight that many men couldn't say that they possessed. Through tough times, and heartbreaks, he still maintained to become a man of his own. There was no better feeling.

After a few hours of spades, laughing, and eating. Chocolate stood up from the table and stretched. "A'ight Boss Man. My ass is tired and I gotta business to run tomorrow so I'm about to leave."

"You know my name girl. We all bosses." He pinched her cheek.

She smiled, grabbed her jacket and headed out. "Later y'all."

Stepping over to Tipton, Rex embraced him. "I would stay and kick it, but I gotta be out too my guy."

"What, nigga where the hell you gotta be?" Tipton said as if he was lying.

"My granny needs to be picked up. You know she be at the old folk's home throughout the day. I can't be changing diapers bro. That ain't no normal shit them folks be pushing out."

Scratching his head, Tipton chuckled. "Please don't explain, I'll see you in the a.m., bro."

"Smooth."

As Rex headed through the patio door to leave. Halo walked over to him. Finishing the last of his Heineken, he tossed the empty glass bottle into the trashcan. "Rex seemed pretty upset earlier, God. I'm guessing you cheered him up?"

"Really? He seemed fine to me."

"He got a phone call earlier, and his entire posture changed. He was acting stiff and angry. I can always sense energy, God. It seemed like he was mad at you."

"One thing I know, Halo. Rex gonna speak on how he feels. He might act like a weenie sometimes, but he means well," Tipton assured.

"Whatever you say, God."

"Besides that, what are you thinking about doing with that paper tomorrow?"

Taking some time to think, Halo quickly canned his idea once again. "I might just save that, God. It's hard to spend money on shit that you don't do. Ever since I been dealing with Sonya my mind has been really wondering."

"You really like her don't it?" Tipton grinned

"I do, God. It's strange how it happened, but I'm a firm believer in things occurring for a reason. She makes me happy, I've never had a woman I can call my girlfriend, but I wanna do that with her."

"I say shoot for what you want, Halo. You deserve that. No one can predict how love will fall. It could be a person you were seconds from killing that eventually becomes a person you will kill off the entire world about. That's just the way things work. But, hey, who's to say you can't build you a family with this girl cause she damn sho ain't going nowhere."

"Most definitely, God. I'm about to get up there to this room before she tries to come look for me." Halo gave him a pound before heading inside.

"Understood."

Not to long after, Tipton made his way inside to relax with Janita for the remainder of the night. As he stepped through the door. She looked at him with a naughty expression.

"I thought that you would be sleep? Were you waiting for me?"

Removing the cover exposing her flawless naked body, she nodded silently. Instead of speaking, Tipton dropped his pants and cut the lights off leaving them in the dark.

Chris Green

Chapter 18

Chocolate stepped out of her shower, placed a towel around her waist and headed inside the kitchen to fix a quick drink of Tequila. Tomorrow was gonna be a big day of splurging, and she wasn't going to sleep anytime soon.

The sharp knock on the front door paused her movements. "What the fuck, who is it?" she yelled.

Receiving no answer, she huffed. She wasn't with the company shit at the time so whoever was there was about to receive the nastiest speech ever. As she opened the front door, the masked man who stood on the other side crashed his gun across her face.

Whamp!

The hit was so forceful it sent Chocolate to the floor. The strength in her body was instantly drained and her hands felt like they were floating in space as she tried to shake her vision clear.

Stepping over her, the man wasted no time beating Chocolate like a disowned dog. He kicked her forcefully in the face.

She grunted in pain, "What did I dooo!" she cried as her head began to bleed profusely.

Ignoring her statement, the attacker continued to strike her in the face with no sympathy. After he realized she was unconscious. He flipped her over and snatched the towel loose exposing her naked body. All she could do was pant for help before he forced himself inside of her anus.

"Aaaggghhh!"

Covering her mouth, he slammed into her roughly. The sound of his deep grunts was all that could be heard throughout her small three-bedroom home. The pain she was feeling forced her to struggle one last time before blanking out on her living room floor.

****

The Next Day: 10:34 a.m.

Sincere pulled inside Tipton's driveway, parked his whip and shut off his engine. Before stepping out he fired up a Newport cigarette. After taking the long drive back from Miami. He prepared himself for the mission that was ahead of him. He never expected to run into the news about Chocolate while passing through the East side of Atlanta. The story caused his stomach to cringe, and he decided to head straight over to Tipton's.

He knocked on the front door and waited for about thirty seconds until his sister opened the home for him to enter.

"Sincere, are you okay?" Janita noticed the depressed look on his face.

"No, where is Tipton?"

"He's in the kitchen with, Halo and Rex. Come in." She stepped to the side.

Passing the threshold, he headed for the crew who sat in deep conversation. Tipton paused his statement to look up at him. "You look sick, my nigga. Is everything good?"

"Nah," Sincere mouthed with a tear dripping down his face.

Sensing the seriousness through his tone. Tipton stood to his feet. "Sincere, what the fuck is going on?"

Halo and Rex sat back quietly waiting for him to speak.

"On my way back from Miami, I passed through the Eastside."

"And?" Tipton said getting aggravated. The pit of his stomach could sense that something was beyond wrong.

The next statement that escaped Sincere's lips caused his heart to crumble in pieces. "They found Chocolate dead. She was burned alive and wrapped inside a blanket. She was killed and found on the street corner around this morning," Sincere said taking a seat at the table.

"What?" Tipton whispered before the tears started to pour from his eyes.

All Sincere could do was nod his head.

Rex stood to his feet and invaded Sincere's personal space. "Tell me you're fucking lying, nigga! Tell me that shit is just a joke!"

"It's not," he replied with a sad expression.

Grabbing one of the kitchen chairs, Rex slammed it forcefully across the wall. "Fuck!"

Janita placed a hand over her mouth in disbelief. Tipton turned his back and glared out of the kitchen window. It was hard for him to take the news. The tears wouldn't stop flowing. Not only was Chocolate apart of his team, but she was also a sister. That was a pain he wouldn't ever be able to let go of.

"I need everything to be put on pause. All movements, I wanna know everybody who had something to do with this!" Tipton clenched his jaws in anger.

"Nigga you know who the fuck did this, Dejuan! He's been running around this bitch ever since you've been home with the fuckery. That bitch is about to die tonight!" Rex yelled before pulling out his gun.

It was the first time Tipton had actually seen his friend hurt, not to mention he was right about Dejuan. The thought of touching his mother and sister flashed through his mind as Rex continued to speak with malice from the heart. It was settled, the boy was like a rabid dog off the leash, and his last straw was officially pulled.

Turning around to face everybody, Tipton wiped his face. "We need to call her family. Aware them if they don't already know. All expenses will be on us, and they shall want for nothing as long as I'm on this earth. That's my dedication to Chocolate as a brother."

"And what about this nigga?" Rex asked, his eyes were fire red.

"Find, Dejuan, bring him to me. Kill all his family. Starting from the oldest to the youngest. None of them should be able to have an open-casket funeral, and I mean that from the bottom of my heart." Tipton looked around at them all.

Halo gazed around at everyone but continued to remain quiet. It was obvious that his friend was hurt dearly, and he surely wasn't about to speak on anything else until they were alone.

"I'm letting you know, right now. I'm not turning back no more, Tip. This was it, he touched the wrong one," Rex stated before heading towards the front door.

"Rex?" Tipton called out.

Turning around to face him, he grabbed the bridge of his nose. "Yeah?"

"Leave him for me. I don't care whoever else you touch. If you find him, bring his ass here!"

Without saying another word. He opened the front door and departed from the crew.

Looking over to Sincere who sat with a worried expression. Tipton folded his arms. "Is that all you know? What else have you heard?"

What do you mean, I just did a successful mission with Kenny and came back, bro. I'm lost like you," he replied nervously.

Eyeing him with suspicion. Tipton dismissed him quickly. "You can leave. Get you some rest and I'll be in contact when it's time to get shit back moving."

"A'ight man." Sincere nodded with relief before rushing out of the front door.

"Baby, I'm so sorry. I know Chocolate was a true friend to you." Janita placed a hand over her heart before hugging his neck.

"It's okay, baby. Regardless of what I say it's not going to bring her back. I'm not stopping until that nigga pay in blood. He took someone that's close to me, and now I'll finish it by taking everything in this world from him."

"I understand, I'll just give you some time alone. I'll be upstairs if you need me." She fidgeted with her fingers before walking off.

Standing to his feet, Halo walked over to Tipton and posted next to him. "Something ain't smelling right about this shit, God. It's not sitting well with me, and I know it's somebody not telling the complete truth. Ever since you told Sincere to make his move with, Kenny. He's been acting weird. The same thing with, Rex. I've never seen him act like that any other time. He and Chocolate didn't even have that type of relationship from what I've seen."

"So, what are you trying to say, Halo?"

"I'm saying we have to always expect the unexpected, God. It's too many feelings floating around to see who's doing what, but somebody has to know something. Think about it, God. Not too many people knew where Chocolate rested. Especially after you warned her about that the first time. I think you need to handle Dejuan first, and do a more thorough investigation."

"I hear you, bro, but right now Dejuan is the main menu. He's been violating for the past six months, and he's never liked, Chocolate. He even raped her when we were younger, on some real psychotic ass sick shit. I know he did it.

Especially with the way we handled his mom and sister."
Tipton rubbed his chin with a positive nod.

"So, what do we do from here, God? He's not gonna come out from hiding if he pulled something dirty like this."

"I'm gonna have patience," Tipton replied before pulling out his phone to make a call.

Chapter 19

One Week Later

As he sat in the seats of the large church, Tipton wiped his eyes from the painful tears that fell from his face. Today was not only a day that he was letting a part of him go, but he was actually burying a friend who meant the world to him. Chocolate's closed casket caused his pain to ache more with every word the pastor spoke. Nothing could stop the evil demons from whispering in his ear. The only thing he pondered on within the past week was revenge. He wanted to take the soul of the one person who caused his dear friend to suffer.

Wrapping a hand around his shoulder. Janita kissed his temple. "It's gonna be okay, baby. I'm right here with you.

The entire church was packed to the highest capacity. Even a few attendants were standing to show their condolences to the black queen. Spotting Peaches' mother sitting on the opposite side of him. Tipton stood up and moved over to her.

She gazed up into his eyes with so much hurt. "How could you have the guts to face me, right here, Tipton, huh?"

Getting on his knees in front of her, he placed both of her hands between his own. "Mama, I never intended for anything to happen to, Chocolate. She's always been my heart, and I promise I won't rest until I find out who did this."

She slapped him across the face. Her tears began to pour harder. "That's because you led her the wrong way from the start. The only reason I'm not mad at you is because ever since you've been a part of my family, I've seen nothing but love and support. You're a great father to my granddaughter, but this isn't anything easy for me to take wit' my old heart. You find the motherfucker that did this to my baby, and you handle him. I mean that shit, you hear me!" she said before pulling him in for a hug.

"Yes mama, I promise," he whispered with his eyes closed.

The sound of the church doors opening caused everyone to look back. When Tipton opened his eyes. The sight of Dejuan sent murderous chills through his body.

"Ain't no way you showed up here, nigga? Are you fucking stupid?" Tipton yelled moving towards him

"Tipton she's my friend, too. I came to show my respect," he replied with his hands in the air.

Removing his pistol, Tipton rushed him with a hard slap to the head sending him to the floor. The entire church began to spiral out of control as the males tried to pull him off Dejuan. Tipton hit him with the pistol repeatedly, causing gashes to form across his face.

"Tip you're gonna fucking kill him in front of everybody. Stop, bro." Rex grabbed ahold of him. "Think about it, wait until we catch his ass. This our sister's funeral, bro," he whispered inside of his ear.

Janita, Halo, and Sincere was directly beside him trying to ease the tension while two more men helped Dejuan off the ground.

"Why y'all stop him! That motherfucker has something to do with my baby being murdered," Peaches mother cried in agony.

"I didn't do it, I didn't fucking do it!" Dejuan yelled at the top of his lungs. "All I wanted you to do was accept me as your friend, nigga. I been right here by your side since middle school."

"Fuck you, boy. You've crossed boundaries beyond your measures, and I don't give a fuck how long it takes. I'ma deal with you. You're not my fucking family. We ain't friends. You took my sister away from me, nigga. You ain't do it? So, I guess you ain't rape Chocolate when we were at the party either, huh?" Holding his head without saying a word. Tipton spit directly in face. "That's what I thought, bitch. When I catch you, yo' ass is dead. Get him the fuck outta here!"

Two of Chocolate's uncles grabbed him by the arms and pushed him back through the church doors. He picked himself up from the hard concrete, then wiped the blood from his mouth and face. There was nothing worse than being blamed for something you didn't do. To make it even harder, the one friend who you felt would come around didn't believe you. Tipton was ready to end Dejuan's life, and that was a feeling that he could never back. What was understood didn't need to be explained. It was either Tipton or him.

****

Four Hours Later

After the burial for Chocolate ended. Tipton checked his phone and spotted the emergency text from Rika. His mind was so distraught about his friend that he didn't even have a chance to distribute his product for the clientele who paid in advance. The only thing that continued to flick through his mind was the statement she made when he was shot months before. "Money means nothing when it comes to you losing somebody you truly care about," the remark continued to eat at his brain because she warned him to get rid of Dejuan before things flipped outta hand.

Not a day that went by would he ever think his best friend would one day flip on him as if they were never tight. His loyalty was so genuine back then, even with the attitude.

Regardless of how much they got into it, he would stand by Tipton's side whether right or wrong. Now those fake ass friendly days were over. Shit was now in a bucket, and the only way out of the mix was a body bag. Still in all, Rika was his connect, and business was something that wouldn't stop.

Tipton pulled into Sleepy's home, parked his car and killed the engine.

Halo unbuckled his seatbelt and looked over at him. "You a'ight, God?

Shaking his head, he sat back. "Sometimes I don't even know anymore, bro. It seems like the bad always outweighs the good. No matter how much honesty, and loyalty we live by. The evil will always overcome."

"That's because it's the only thing we're used to, God. We live to learn and grow. No matter what friends you could've had back then. It wouldn't change what's decreed for us."

"But that wasn't what I was used too. I grew up experiencing all the love from Ma Dukes. She gave me the world, but she also showed me that this motherfucka can have different ups and downs. Out of my twenty-one years of being on this fucking earth, I've never felt so low. The ones who we trust with our lives will flip and be the same one to take it away from us. How can you trust anyone if you feel that way, bro?"

"Because, God, you have no choice. If we don't trust somebody, we'll eventually turn on ourselves. Trust was made for us to accept people into our lives. Either for a small amount of time or for eternity. That's the only true way you will ever know if somebody truly cares. When we were younger in school, people became your friends by talking and going through certain experiences with you. If they never took the step to build that relationship. That would be one less person that you could say wasn't trustworthy. You never know until you try, God. As I said, I have no explaining when it comes to my loyalty. I'm here for you until my days are over."

Tipton gave Halo a pound and a smile. They both stepped out of the car and headed inside. It didn't take long before the butler granted them access by opening the front door.

As he headed for the living room, Sleepy stood to his feet with a huge smile once the guys stepped into his line of vision. "Tipton, all I can say is bravo son."

"Really? What do I deserve the applause for," he replied showing Sleepy some love with a handshake.

"Because you're the only person I've ever seen to out beat your mother at her own hustle."

'What do you mean?" Tipton asked confused.

"Simple, your mother was the only person to place Georgia on lock with her recipe. You have risen pass that by taking three."

"What's the difference? It's just two more states."

"There's a big difference. It took your mother two years to take the entire Georgia. It took you two weeks to conquer three. I've received over six phone calls today about more product. Kima is sitting on her ass watching her money stack faster than she's ever seen before. Milo is begging for another shipment, not to mention the twenty-man crew that your men hired while in Omaha. They've wired me half of a million dollars within three days. Your workers have taken the recipe and showed out. Biggs, on the other hand, he's just gonna be Biggs," Sleepy said with a nonchalant smirk."

"Facts, I like to hear things like that. It's gonna be even bigger when I take Miami. All we need is a seed that can expand through the entire land, and we will win."

"Exactly that's the reason why I'm handing down my throne soon. I'm leaving the connect with you, and I'm guaranteed that things will still flourish tremendously."

Chris Green

"What do you mean? You're quitting for good?" Tipton questioned.

"Yes, my time with the game is over. You've come in and made numbers I've never seen. Even when your mother was with me. It's in your blood to be the boss, Tipton. No one else. Everybody is not meant for control. I'm sure you will be able to hold a balance of some sort with this foundation."

Thinking to himself, Chocolate flashed through his mind. "I just buried somebody very close to me today, and no matter how much I believe that you're right. I feel this game claimed her life. Hopefully, I can take up that offer, but I would like a few days to sit and ponder on that."

Nodding with understanding, Sleepy placed a hand on his shoulder. "I see, I want you to know something. When we step in this world there is never a guarantee that everyone will make it out. It's the reason you put leaders and thinkers in charge. Not the arrogant, and deadly. You are a mastermind with your hustle. You were meant to have this seat. Think smart about your actions also because I know that losing loved ones can make us do things we will regret in the near future. Never let anyone disturb your comfort and know that you will survive."

Embracing Tipton with a hug, Sleepy patted him on the back. "Come see me soon." He smirked.

"I will. Thank you, for everything," he replied before heading out of the home with Halo by his side.

Rika stepped out of the front door behind him. "Tipton?"

Looking back into her beautiful face, he smiled. "Hey, Rika."

She strolled over to him, placing a passionate kiss on his lips. "I'm sorry for your loss, and I'll always be here if you need me. You can come and stay whenever you want."

Chuckling from her forwardness, he squeezed her hand.

"Thank you, Rika. I'll be sure to come and see you soon. I promise," he whispered before walking off.

He got inside the car with Halo and smirked. "Have you ever wondered how it feels to be a millionaire, bro?"

"Tell you the truth, nah, God. I never really cared. Status of money only means that people are gonna talk about you a little less and ask for a whole lot more. I'm good on all the fake love."

"Exactly, sometimes you don't have to know that you a millionaire in order to be one. Maybe it's best to keep the money a secret from yourself to not aware the beggars and talkers. I guess that's something that'll always be in the midst until we all grow on handling certain things," Tipton said before starting the car.

****

Driving down the street in his junkie rental, Dejuan eyed the large dried up cuts on his face through the mirror. The black eye he received earlier still had his head thumping with pain every time he blinked. It wasn't like him to accept the shit Tipton did. But how the fuck could a nigga beat an entire church full of angry ass fake people. Nothing was better than revenge though. It was all funny when he was getting his ass kicked left and right, but people wouldn't be laughing when they found Tipton's entire crew dead. The most hurtful part about the shitty situation was nobody approached him as a friend and asked about the situation with him and Chocolate on the night of her house party. She came on to him and acted as if she didn't want to fuck because of Tipton being in the same house. He still remembered her words till that exact day.

"No, I'm not gonna have sex with you while Tipton's here, Dejuan. It's disrespectful," the statement made no sense, especially when Tipton wasn't feeling her at all when it came down to locking in with a girl. It caused him to overreact and force himself on her. Even though it wasn't right. He knew his heart couldn't respect the fact of Chocolate putting him on pause for a nigga that didn't give two cents about her ass. It hurt, even more, to know his best friend thought that he murdered her. In the end, there was nothing else to prove. It was the last time he would try to give an explanation about anything. Tipton's ass was gonna die, and nothing would ever change that.

He pulled inside the small gas station on his right-hand side. Dejuan parked and stepped out of the car. His phone began to ring stopping his motion. "Hello?" he answered while rubbing the scar on his forehead.

"Juan?" Peaches spoke through the line.

"What man!"

"Nigga don't yell at me cause I didn't do shit to you. I was just letting you know that word around town is Tipton's putting three-hundred gees on your head for anybody that can bring you to him."

"Bitch how the fuck you hear some shit like that if you ain't fucking with this, nigga?" he spazzed.

"Stop yelling dumb ass, I heard my uncles and mama discussing it after Chocolate's funeral today. He's dead ass serious, Juan. He thinks you killed her," Peaches warned.

"Don't you think I know that shit. I'm not letting nobody do shit to me. You calling my phone like you trying to set me up or some hoe."

"Juan, I'm not trying to do anything to yo' dumb ass. I know you didn't kill my cousin, but I can't keep beefing with my baby daddy because of you. I'm tired of not being able to see my baby. I need him."

"What! So, what happened to me and you?"

"Juan, I'm leaving. My daughter means more to me than all this bullshit. I just lost my cousin and I'm not trying to leave my baby. I'm sorry," she said sincerely.

"Bitch, after all the shit I did for you?"

Before he could continue his rant. The sound of numerous tires screeching around him broke his attention. The four cop cars that surrounded him came to a halt, and all the officers stepped out with their guns drawn. "Mr. Dejuan Williams put your hands up in the air son. You're under arrest!"

Wasting no time, he jolted off. Running quickly on the side of the corner store. He could hear the bullets rang out from the officer's gun. Tripping up, he fell and scrambled back to his feet without looking back. The sound of walkie talkies was surely at a small distance, and there weren't no chances of making it out of the sticky situation if he didn't run with everything he got.

Kicking off his shoes, he began to pick up the pace. The bushes he was running through slapped him clean in the face before he bumped into a giant bob wire fence. Wasting no time, he began to climb until he reached the top. He could see the small group of cops gaining on him from a distance. Holding his breath, he brushed over the sharp razors slicing his arms and back instantly before hitting the ground, jumping to his feet. The sound of loud thunder quaked through the sky. Feeling the burns of his fresh cut, he still ran with a mission to escape.

The slight drizzle of rain coming down could surely buy him some time. Especially when he was trying to dodge the slimy ass cops who was sure to catch him by the dog, or helicopter. After another two minutes of jogging through the middle of nowhere, the heavy rain began to pour. His socks became mushy, and his clothes became soaked.

Dejuan stepped out of a cut and stared up at the street sign that read Gresham Road. It wasn't home, but it was close enough to know exactly where he was. It was either now or never. All he had to do was make it down to the nearest hotel, and he would be home free. He looked both ways and sprung back into action.

****

"You know, God. We ain't never had a chance to really build with the people who be around us. That's part of the reason we never know who's on what page," Halo said as him and Tipton drove through the late-night rain.

"Yeah, I know. From now on we just gonna rock alone and keep the rest working. It's just business, I'm starting not to trust people anymore, Halo. I don't give a damn how long I been knowing them," Tipton replied while looking out of the window.

His intentions were so focused on starting over that he literally thought his mind was playing tricks on him. The sight of Dejuan running down the street sent his radar sky high.

"Halo is that who the fuck I think it is?"

Looking to his right, he stared at the back of Dejuan's head as he sprinted smoothly down the street in the rain as if shit was normal. "If you referring to that slimeball ass friend. That's definitely him."

Removing his pistol, Tipton placed one in the chamber. "Pull down on his ass!"

Jumping into action, Halo mashed the gas. "Do you want me to run him over, God?"

"Nah, just get me close enough to where he can't run," Tipton said with thirst in his tone for blood.

****

Hearing the acceleration of a car flying behind him. Dejuan tried to pick up his pace. He glanced back, began to realize that the vehicle wasn't a police cruiser. Just as he thought about slowing down, the car came to a halt and Tipton surfaced from the passenger side with his pistol aimed.

The feeling in his stomach began to grow tight and he knew that his luck couldn't get any worse. Fleeing down into the small alley directly next to him. He jumped over the broken glass, and bags of trash. His movements ceased when he realized he was inside of a dead end.

He walked slowly through the cut. Tipton moved towards him with a look of death written on his face. The sight of Halo parking in front of the alley and stepping out caused him to look around for something to protect himself. His gun was stuck inside the car, and now he was face to face with the same person who wanted him deleted from the earth.

He raised his hands in fear and stared into Tipton's low brown eyes. "So, is this what it's comes down to, nigga. I'm still your brother!" Dejuan shouted as the raindrops bounced off his face.

"You ain't shit to me, boy! I fed you pussy. I gave you half of everything I had. When you were broke, I made sure you were straight, and you turned around and still backstabbed me!"

"I didn't fucking kill her, nigga. I swear, Tip, I just wanted you to listen to me, bro. You're my brother, I've never held nothing from you since we first met. Rex was the cause of all this shit, my nigga. He got us beefing like this!" Dejuan shouted truthfully with his hands in the air.

"Shut the fuck up, bitch. Rex ain't got shit to do with this!"

Halo stood at the front of the alley listening to every word.

"Yes, he does, bro. Rex is lying to you. That nigga blew

all your money when you was down, bro. Think about it. You left him a hundred grand of your paper and you came back home to an extra twenty-five thousand. That was me, I ran that shit back up for you, Tip. He blew through your shit and didn't have anything to show for it. I got that paper back so you could come home to something, bro. That nigga robbed Shaggy fool. I wouldn't be surprised if it wasn't that nigga who killed, Chocolate. He's a fucking snake, and you won't believe me, bro. This is the reason why I spazzed out. That nigga don't love you for real, but he got you thinking that he the realest friend ever."

"You a fucking liar, I don't believe you. You can't give me one reason to back up your statement. Say it, nigga, tell me why should I believe you," Tipton stressed putting the gun to Dejuan's mouth.

"Because I've never had the courage to even try you like that. I tell you the truth no matter what. Yes, I killed Lisa because that bitch lied to you. She told you that I put her on dope. Nigga that was, Rex. All I did was keep serving her. She wasn't your real auntie, nigga. I was more of family to you than her. Why do you think she never came to see you, bro. Or the way she never wrote you. It was all because of Rex throwing salt on your name nigga."

Shaking his head, Tipton grew angrier. "I don't believe none of that shit!"

Touching his shoulder, Halo nodded. "Just hear him out, God."

"Fuck that, I'm done hearing this nigga out. You crossed me, bro. Even if what you saying is true. You made it this way. All you had to do was rock, nigga. To be a fucking friend and remain loyal. Was that hard? Huh!" Tipton shouted before hitting him with the gun.

The rain was beginning to pick back up, and now Dejuan

was sitting on the ground looking up into his best friend's eyes. "You won't be a man if you kill me, bro. You'll just be a murderer because I never did it, Tip. I never did it," he pleaded with sad eyes.

Tipton pulled the trigger, one slug landed directly in the center of Dejuan's skull causing Halo to jump. As he stared down at his friend's lifeless body. He lowered his head and headed back for the car. As he followed behind him, Halo held his statement until they were back in the car. "I don't feel right, God."

Tipton sat in the driver's seat cutting his eyes over at him. "What do you mean, bro?"

"That what just happened, God, it wasn't right. I can feel it in my gut. I'm never wrong when it comes down to shit like this."

"Nigga, what the fuck you trying to say?" Tipton clutched onto his gun with a raised eyebrow.

"God, calm the fuck down. I've been doing this for a long time. The things he was saying made sense. Think about it. Rex comes up missing every time this slime shit is going on, or he happens to be around the next day in order to cover his ass. His movements have always been funny to me since I first met him. That nigga's a weed junkie, God. You said your plug was robbed. Nobody, but Dejuan and Rex knew about his location. What did Rex tell you when you asked him?"

"He blamed it on Dejuan," Tipton mumbled.

"Exactly, not only that, everything you've questioned him about since I've been home with you. He's blamed it on, Dejuan. I don't think he was lying, God. The feelings I get are never wrong," Halo said staring inside the dark alley.

He put the car in drive, Tipton slammed his hands on the steering wheel forcefully. "So, what you think we should do now. We might as well just kill everybody?"

"Nah, God, it's deeper than that. It's something else going on. I've never met a dude like Rex before. He's hiding something, and if I'm wrong, I'll take my punishment in the hereafter. You have to open your eyes and view things from every angle."

Tipton's phone began to ring before he could reply. He grabbed it out of the center console and answered. "Yeah?"

"Uh, hey baby. When are you coming home?"

"I'm on the way, right now, Janita. Is everything okay?"

"Uh, yeah, there's some people waiting in the living room for you. They said they need to have a conversation about unhandled business."

"What? Janita, I know you didn't let nobody in our home? Who the fuck is it?" Tipton screwed up his face.

"I don't know, baby. I didn't let them in. They were sitting in the living room when I got home," she whispered through the line.

Chapter 20

Tipton pulled the car inside of their driveway. He and Halo jumped out of the whip with their guns in hand. They stared at the six black BMW 745s. He moved towards the front door. It was no telling what to expect when they entered, so Halo wasted no time stepping in front of Tipton in case shit got ugly.

Halo and Tipton entered the front door and witnessed seven gunmen dressed in black suits posted around his living room. All of them were draped in dress shoes and red ties. Their posture still remained the same as if Tipton and Halo were visitors inside their own home.

"Well, hello?" A woman dressed in a black dress spoke with a light voice.

Her blonde hair was curly hanging gently down her back. Her healthy body was magnificent in the tight-fitting fabric. Her eyes were a tad bit shade darker than Halo's and her luscious lips were coated with red lipstick.

"Who the fuck are you?" Tipton said while clutching his gun.

Before he could speak, Janita stepped through the living room with a few drinks in her hand. The sight of Tipton caused her to exhale in relief.

The woman stood to her feet and grabbed a drink from Janita's hand. "Thank you, darling," she said before moving towards Tipton. "My name is Lotus. You are the man in charge correct?" She placed a hand on his shoulder.

Before she could speak again, Halo placed his pistol up to her forehead.

The armed men in the room didn't hesitate to return the gesture by snatching up Janita and pointing their weapons also.

"I think we just got off to a very bad start." Lotus smiled as if Halo's pistol wasn't connecting to her skin. "Maybe you need to tell your blue-eyed friend to relax, Tipton?"

"Baby!" Janita mumbled as one of the guards held her by the throat.

"Halo, relax."

"Nah, God, I've had enough of this shit today. Tell your men to put their guns down or I'll blow your head off."

Exhaling, she smirked. "We can all be friends ya know. I didn't come to harm anyone."

Her older brother Jax sat back against the wall with his mouth sealed. The tattoo of a black snake was wrapped around his eye. If he wanted too, he could kill the entire room with his bare hands. Instead, he decided to see how things were gonna play before releasing the beast.

She snapped her fingers at the armed men. They released Janita and lowered their weapons.

Halo continued to hold his position with his finger on the trigger as he gazed into Lotus's eyes, biting his bottom lip.

"Halo, chill the fuck out. Please bro." Tipton placed a hand on his shoulder to calm his nerves.

Lowering his gun, he stood close by Tipton just in case things got ugly.

"Now that we are not so uptight I can explain why I'm here." Lotus smiled.

"Great, because that's what I'm waiting to hear," Tipton said angrily.

Lotus sat back down on his couch and crossed her leg exposing the black snake that was going down her thigh. "You may not know me, but you were pretty close to my brother."

"Who is your brother?"

"Shaggy," she replied before sipping her wine. "Now I'm only here for one reason to find out where is the man who harmed him. See we aren't the average people, regardless of how much of a fuck up, my little brother was. My mother is angered about his death, and we are willing to kill everything in sight until we find him."

Shaking his head with a disappointing face, Tipton folded his arms. "I loved Shaggy as if he was my own brother. I was in prison when he was killed, and it's still a few answers that I'm looking for on that matter also. I'm sorry to inform you on that, but there's not much I can say. I don't know who did it."

"Oh, no, you're not hearing me clearly darling. Let me be more distinct. I know who killed my brother. I'm looking for him, and you are going to be the one who leads me to him," she said with assurance.

"What, how can I lead you to someone I don't know?"

Snapping her finger, she reached for the camera in her bodyguard's hand. "Take a look yourself."

He reached for the small device in her hand. Tipton stared at the recorded video.

The sight of Rex's car was sitting in Shaggy's driveway, and from the looks of it. Kimmi was asleep in the backseat, watching the masked man walk out of the house. He placed two black bags in the trunk and jumped inside the vehicle. He rotated his eyes down to the license plate solidified it all. It was surely Rex's license plate on film leaving out the driveway on the day of Shaggy's murder.

"You look as if you may have an idea who that man is? To be honest, it was quite easy to get a picture of him. It sucks when you pull a murder in a car that's registered in your name."

"Can you give me second please?" Tipton said pulling Halo to the side.

"Sure." She smiled before taking another sip from her

169

glass.

"What is it, God?"

"It's fucking, Rex. That's his car on the video. I'd know that nigga from anywhere. He can have on a coat, mask, or whatever and I'll still be able to recognize him. He's the one who killed, Shaggy."

Lowering his head, Halo instantly thought about Dejuan. "I told you something didn't feel right, God."

Pulling out his phone, Tipton quickly typed his slime ass number into the phone and pressed the dial button. As he listened to the line buzz in his ear, Rex picked up on the third ring. "Waddup?"

"You pussy ass motherfucker! You killed Shaggy, and you've been lying this entire time. You slimed me out, stole money from me and betrayed to be my friend. I trusted you like a fucking brother, and this is how you repay me? I guess you killed Chocolate too, huh?"

"Smooth," Rex replied before hanging up in his ear.

Feeling his heart drop, he knew at that moment. Dejuan's life was taken for no reason. He even recited a small prayer in his head to be forgiven for his transgression. Still in all, it would never bring him back, and the new snake was a man he trusted over everyone around him. The only question he kept asking himself was, why?

He placed the phone back into his pocket and stepped back over to Lotus with a disturbed expression.

"I take it you're not too happy about that phone call?" She gazed into his eyes with no sympathy.

"Nah, I'm not, but that doesn't change the fact of our situation. It seems you've shown me something about my crew that I wasn't aware of. Not only do I hate snakes, but I don't tolerate a motherfucker touching anybody that holds a place in my heart. I promise you I'm going to deal with him personally."

"No, you won't." She stood to her feet and moved closer to him until they stood face to face. "This is a sad point of time for you and I can understand that. It must feel so bad to know that you've had a trader hiding under the grass for so long. Unfortunately, I'm not here to have any empathy for that. My family would like to deal with him privately. This is family we're speaking on, not a friend. Maybe after it's done, and you help lead him to me. You can come see me personally if you wanna get a little anger of your chest," she whispered into his ear seductively.

"I'll be sure to keep you updated." Tipton stared into her eyes with a nonchalant smirk.

She snapped her fingers and brushed her ass against him before heading out of the home. Halo stepped to the side as the men began to pile out of Tipton's crib. His hand was still clutching on the gun just in case anyone made a false move. Her brother Jax was the last one to walk past them. He sized Halo up with a smile before spitting on the living room floor.

"Let me just kill him, God," he begged.

Holding up a hand to silence him, Tipton waited until the man exited his home, and closed the door behind them. "I know how you're feeling, right now, but I'm just as hot, bro. We have a serious problem on our hands, and I'm gonna need your help more than anything. We need to find this bitch and take care of this shit quickly. It's understood what he's done, and now I truly regret doing what I did tonight. On the strength of, Dejuan, I'm gonna take care of him."

"What are we supposed to do, God? They don't want us to handle him, and he's definitely not gonna come willingly."

"That doesn't mean we can't damn near kill him before they finish his ass off," Tipton said with a stern look on his face. "Janita call Peaches, Mama, and let her know we're coming to get Kimmi tonight. We're getting y'all out of here until this is squashed."

"Okay." She moved quickly pulling her cell out of the Gucci purse on the table.

"I knew that nigga was a snake, God. It was always something about him. He was never your friend. I learned at a young age that the one who smiles too much in your face, that's the one who will frown wit' hatred when you walk off. You have to take care of this idiot quick before he gets out of control. Now that he knows, he's gonna try to show out," Halo warned."

"Fuck it, we're on his ass. From his family, down to his closest associates," Tipton replied.

"Uh, baby? We got a problem," Janita said with a worried look.

"What do you mean? What's wrong?" He and Halo paused their conversation.

"Peaches mama said that Kimmi isn't there."

"What the fuck do you mean my daughter ain't there? Where the hell is, she?" Tipton snapped instantly.

Stumbling with her words, Janita held down her head. "She said Rex just came and picked her up twenty minutes ago."

To Be Continued...
Dope Boy Magic 3
Coming Soon

Submission Guideline

Submit the first three chapters of your completed manuscript to ldpsubmissions@gmail.com, subject line: Your book's title. The manuscript must be in a .doc file and sent as an attachment. Document should be in Times New Roman, double spaced and in size 12 font. Also, provide your synopsis and full contact information. If sending multiple submissions, they must each be in a separate email.

Have a story but no way to send it electronically? You can still submit to LDP/Ca$h Presents. Send in the first three chapters, written or typed, of your completed manuscript to:

LDP: Submissions Dept
Po Box 870494
Mesquite, Tx 75187

DO NOT send original manuscript. Must be a duplicate.

Provide your synopsis and a cover letter containing your full contact information.

Thanks for considering LDP and Ca$h Presents.

Chris Green

Coming Soon from Lock Down Publications/Ca$h Presents

BOW DOWN TO MY GANGSTA

By **Ca$h**

TORN BETWEEN TWO

By **Coffee**

THE STREETS STAINED MY SOUL **II**

By **Marcellus Allen**

BLOOD OF A BOSS **VI**

SHADOWS OF THE GAME II

By **Askari**

LOYAL TO THE GAME **IV**

By **T.J. & Jelissa**

A DOPEBOY'S PRAYER **II**

By **Eddie "Wolf" Lee**

IF LOVING YOU IS WRONG... **III**

By **Jelissa**

TRUE SAVAGE **VII**

MIDNIGHT CARTEL II

DOPE BOY MAGIC III

By **Chris Green**

BLAST FOR ME **III**

DUFFLE BAG CARTEL **IV**

HEARTLESS GOON **IV**

A SAVAGE DOPEBOY II

DRUG LORDS III

By **Ghost**

A HUSTLER'S DECEIT III

KILL ZONE **II**

BAE BELONGS TO ME III

SOUL OF A MONSTER III

By **Aryanna**

THE COST OF LOYALTY **III**

By **Kweli**

THE SAVAGE LIFE III

CHAINED TO THE STREETS II

By **J-Blunt**

KING OF NEW YORK V

COKE KINGS IV

BORN HEARTLESS IV

By **T.J. Edwards**

GORILLAZ IN THE BAY V

De'Kari

THE STREETS ARE CALLING II

Duquie Wilson

KINGPIN KILLAZ IV

STREET KINGS III

PAID IN BLOOD III

CARTEL KILLAZ IV

Hood Rich

SINS OF A HUSTLA II

ASAD

TRIGGADALE III

Elijah R. Freeman

Chris Green

KINGZ OF THE GAME V
Playa Ray
SLAUGHTER GANG IV
RUTHLESS HEART II
By Willie Slaughter
THE HEART OF A SAVAGE II
By Jibril Williams
FUK SHYT II
By Blakk Diamond
THE DOPEMAN'S BODYGAURD II
By Tranay Adams
TRAP GOD II
By Troublesome
YAYO III
A SHOOTER'S AMBITION II
By S. Allen
GHOST MOB
Stilloan Robinson
KINGPIN DREAMS II
By Paper Boi Rari
CREAM
By Yolanda Moore
SON OF A DOPE FIEND II
By Renta
FOREVER GANGSTA II
By Adrian Dulan
LOYALTY AIN'T PROMISED

By Keith Williams

THE PRICE YOU PAY FOR LOVE II

By Destiny Skai

THE LIFE OF A HOOD STAR

By Rashia Wilson

TOE TAGZ II

By Ah'Million

CONFESSIONS OF A GANGSTA II

By Nicholas Lock

PAID IN KARMA II

By **Meesha**

<u>Available Now</u>

RESTRAINING ORDER **I & II**

By **CA$H & Coffee**

LOVE KNOWS NO BOUNDARIES **I II & III**

By **Coffee**

RAISED AS A GOON I, II, III & IV

BRED BY THE SLUMS I, II, III

BLAST FOR ME I & II

ROTTEN TO THE CORE I II III

A BRONX TALE I, II, III

DUFFEL BAG CARTEL I II III

HEARTLESS GOON

A SAVAGE DOPEBOY

HEARTLESS GOON I II III

Chris Green

DRUG LORDS I II

By **Ghost**

LAY IT DOWN **I & II**

LAST OF A DYING BREED

BLOOD STAINS OF A SHOTTA I & II III

By **Jamaica**

LOYAL TO THE GAME

LOYAL TO THE GAME II

LOYAL TO THE GAME III

LIFE OF SIN I, II III

By **TJ & Jelissa**

BLOODY COMMAS I & II

SKI MASK CARTEL I II & III

KING OF NEW YORK I II,III IV

RISE TO POWER I II III

COKE KINGS I II III

BORN HEARTLESS I II III

By **T.J. Edwards**

IF LOVING HIM IS WRONG…I & II

LOVE ME EVEN WHEN IT HURTS I II III

By **Jelissa**

WHEN THE STREETS CLAP BACK I & II III

By **Jibril Williams**

A DISTINGUISHED THUG STOLE MY HEART I II & III

LOVE SHOULDN'T HURT I II III IV

RENEGADE BOYS I II III IV

PAID IN KARMA

178

By **Meesha**

A GANGSTER'S CODE I &, II III

A GANGSTER'S SYN I II III

THE SAVAGE LIFE I II

CHAINED TO THE STREETS

By J-Blunt

PUSH IT TO THE LIMIT

By **Bre' Hayes**

BLOOD OF A BOSS **I, II, III, IV, V**

SHADOWS OF THE GAME

By **Askari**

THE STREETS BLEED MURDER **I, II & III**

THE HEART OF A GANGSTA I II& III

By **Jerry Jackson**

CUM FOR ME

CUM FOR ME 2

CUM FOR ME 3

CUM FOR ME 4

CUM FOR ME 5

An **LDP Erotica Collaboration**

BRIDE OF A HUSTLA **I II & II**

THE FETTI GIRLS **I, II& III**

CORRUPTED BY A GANGSTA I, II III, IV

BLINDED BY HIS LOVE

THE PRICE YOU PAY FOR LOVE

By **Destiny Skai**

WHEN A GOOD GIRL GOES BAD

Chris Green

By **Adrienne**
THE COST OF LOYALTY I II
By Kweli
A GANGSTER'S REVENGE **I II III & IV**
THE BOSS MAN'S DAUGHTERS
THE BOSS MAN'S DAUGHTERS II
THE BOSSMAN'S DAUGHTERS III
THE BOSSMAN'S DAUGHTERS IV
THE BOSS MAN'S DAUGHTERS **V**
A SAVAGE LOVE **I & II**
BAE BELONGS TO ME I II
A HUSTLER'S DECEIT I, II, III
WHAT BAD BITCHES DO I, II, III
SOUL OF A MONSTER I II
KILL ZONE
By **Aryanna**
A KINGPIN'S AMBITON
A KINGPIN'S AMBITION **II**
I MURDER FOR THE DOUGH
By **Ambitious**
TRUE SAVAGE
TRUE SAVAGE II
TRUE SAVAGE **III**
TRUE SAVAGE **IV**
TRUE SAVAGE **V**
TRUE SAVAGE **VI**
DOPE BOY MAGIC I, II

MIDNIGHT CARTEL

By **Chris Green**

A DOPEBOY'S PRAYER

By **Eddie "Wolf" Lee**

THE KING CARTEL **I, II & III**

By **Frank Gresham**

THESE NIGGAS AIN'T LOYAL **I, II & III**

By **Nikki Tee**

GANGSTA SHYT **I II &III**

By **CATO**

THE ULTIMATE BETRAYAL

By **Phoenix**

BOSS'N UP **I , II & III**

By **Royal Nicole**

I LOVE YOU TO DEATH

By Destiny J

I RIDE FOR MY HITTA

I STILL RIDE FOR MY HITTA

By **Misty Holt**

LOVE & CHASIN' PAPER

By **Qay Crockett**

TO DIE IN VAIN

SINS OF A HUSTLA

By **ASAD**

BROOKLYN HUSTLAZ

By **Boogsy Morina**

BROOKLYN ON LOCK I & II

Chris Green

By **Sonovia**

GANGSTA CITY

By **Teddy Duke**

A DRUG KING AND HIS DIAMOND I & II III

A DOPEMAN'S RICHES

HER MAN, MINE'S TOO I, II

CASH MONEY HO'S

By Nicole Goosby

TRAPHOUSE KING **I II & III**

KINGPIN KILLAZ I II III

STREET KINGS I II

PAID IN BLOOD **I II**

CARTEL KILLAZ I II III

By **Hood Rich**

LIPSTICK KILLAH **I, II, III**

CRIME OF PASSION I II & III

By **Mimi**

STEADY MOBBN' **I, II, III**

THE STREETS STAINED MY SOUL

By **Marcellus Allen**

WHO SHOT YA **I, II, III**

SON OF A DOPE FIEND

Renta

GORILLAZ IN THE BAY **I II III IV**

DE'KARI

TRIGGADALE I II

Elijah R. Freeman

182

Dope Boy Magic 2

GOD BLESS THE TRAPPERS I, II, III

THESE SCANDALOUS STREETS I, II, III

FEAR MY GANGSTA I, II, III

THESE STREETS DON'T LOVE NOBODY I, II

BURY ME A G I, II, III, IV, V

A GANGSTA'S EMPIRE I, II, III, IV

THE DOPEMAN'S BODYGAURD

Tranay Adams

THE STREETS ARE CALLING

Duquie Wilson

MARRIED TO A BOSS… I II III

By Destiny Skai & Chris Green

KINGZ OF THE GAME I II III IV

Playa Ray

SLAUGHTER GANG I II III

RUTHLESS HEART

By Willie Slaughter

THE HEART OF A SAVAGE

By Jibril Williams

FUK SHYT

By Blakk Diamond

DON'T F#CK WITH MY HEART I II

By Linnea

ADDICTED TO THE DRAMA I II III

By Jamila

YAYO I II

A SHOOTER'S AMBITION

Chris Green

By S. Allen
TRAP GOD
By Troublesome
FOREVER GANGSTA
By Adrian Dulan
TOE TAGZ
By Ah'Million
KINGPIN DREAMS
By Paper Boi Rari
CONFESSIONS OF A GANGSTA
By Nicholas Lock

BOOKS BY LDP'S CEO, CA$H

TRUST IN NO MAN

TRUST IN NO MAN 2

TRUST IN NO MAN 3

BONDED BY BLOOD

SHORTY GOT A THUG

THUGS CRY

THUGS CRY 2

THUGS CRY 3

TRUST NO BITCH

TRUST NO BITCH 2

TRUST NO BITCH 3

TIL MY CASKET DROPS

RESTRAINING ORDER

RESTRAINING ORDER 2

IN LOVE WITH A CONVICT

Coming Soon

BONDED BY BLOOD 2

BOW DOWN TO MY GANGSTA

Chris Green

www.ingramcontent.com/pod-product-compliance
Lightning Source LLC
Chambersburg PA
CBHW070519260626
47161CB00004B/1589